LOVE HOLLOW AT LAST

EVE T MIZUNO

1

———

Aya knew the bulldozer would arrive at dawn, but she wasn't sure she could wake up early enough to handcuff herself to the damn thing—or whether she would be arrested.

It would have been a beautiful morning to burst out her door, run to the mountain bike, and take off in the cool summer air. Unfortunately, she had to wake Emi, who never got up early unless she had to work.

"I don't know why you're doing this, Aya," complained Emi, burrowing into the small couch. "I had enough early mornings during residency to last me a lifetime."

"So you should be good at it," said Aya, zipping up her jacket as she poked her friend's shoulder.

"No," said Emi firmly. "This is my vacation."

"Come on," begged Aya. "Don't you want to see me in leopard-print handcuffs?"

They were all she had been able to find at the last minute.

The lump on the couch stirred. "Yes," said Emi. "Actually, I do."

The sky was already turning pink as they left. The mountains surrounding the town of Love Hollow were still dark, but the stars were no longer visible, and the dog walkers were already out.

Aya fiddled with the handcuffs in her pocket. For all her bravado, she was secretly terrified of getting arrested. Since she was already low on funds, the idea of not even being able to get a low-earning job was terrifying.

Emi, apparently unbothered by those thoughts, was still yawning. "I mean, I know you liked to sit on that rock, but it's just a rock."

Aya was not going to share her reasons. It was *not* just a rock, but the rock itself didn't matter anymore. So much more was at stake.

"Let's go," she urged her friend. "If we miss it, they'll start driving the bulldozer around, and we'll have to catch it."

Emi laughed. "I am *not* chasing a bulldozer. If we're late, this is off."

When they arrived, Aya took out zip ties. They would be less impressive, but she just couldn't face the thought of leopard-print handcuffs. Construction had been happening for weeks, but as obnoxious as the tents and stages might be, at least they would go away once the crowds did. The rock, the one with the perfect view of her past, where she had once been able to sit and imagine a beautiful future... If they took that away, it would be gone forever.

And again, Aya reminded herself, it wasn't about the rock. It was about her family's history. She pulled out a little baggie of zip ties, noting in dismay that they were pretty thin. Maybe she could pull the sleeves of her hoodie down a bit so that wouldn't be as noticeable.

Emi made her own zip ties so loose that she was able to easily slip her hands in and out. "That's it," she said. "Aya, you need to wear the handcuffs."

Aya grumbled, but she was secretly glad she was the one who would wear them. If Aya ended up trapped with a bulldozer, at least Emi's hands would be free for a rescue.

"Can you cover them with my sleeves a little bit?" Aya asked. "That way, the pattern won't be so obvious."

"I would murder someone for a cup of coffee right now," Emi said, grinning as she pointedly ignored Aya's instructions.

It was barely dawn, and the sun rising over the mountains was a sight that never failed to touch something in Aya's soul. She was sure there had been sunrises when she was in Boston, but she certainly never noticed any of them.

"I have coffee," said Twyla, strolling over with a huge grin on her face. No matter what she was doing, Twyla always looked like she was dancing. She still had the permanent turnout common with former ballerinas, and her lithe frame had a knack of making even the most casual clothes look fantastic.

"Twy," groaned Aya. "Go away! Nobody is going to take our protest seriously if you're here with a latte."

Twyla raised her eyes. "I'll have you know this is a thermos full of coffee I made myself. Not some fancy schmancy latte. But I suppose I don't have to give you any."

Emi was pretending to be serious. "Yeah, you'd better not have any, Aya. What if you need to pee?"

"What if you do?" asked Aya, glaring as Twyla twisted off the top of her thermos and filled it up for Emi.

Emi pulled a hand out of the zip tie, waggled it around,

then put it back through. "That's why you keep these things loose, champ."

"Seriously," Aya begged. "Twy, you have to leave."

"You should be telling me to stay. If the local press doesn't show up to cover the story, did it even happen?"

"I really think you have a conflict of interest here."

She lowered her voice. "Of course I do! I'm a huge Noah Kato fan. The man, the music, the magic. Speak of the devil!"

She looked over her shoulder, and Aya whipped her head around.

Oblivious to Twyla's and Emi's reactions, she stared at the man. *Shouldn't the person who's supposed to operate the bulldozer be arriving first? Why is Noah striding toward us, looking both more casual and more handsome than he ever has in his music videos, smiling ever so slightly?*

"L-Ladies," he said. "Good morning."

N oah

Strangers often thought Noah stuttered because he was nervous. But other people who stuttered knew it was the other way around. Because Noah stuttered, it made him nervous. Sometimes, it made him *very* nervous.

But as he gazed at the bulldozer, stuttering receded into the background. He had many other reasons for him to feel nervous.

He recognized the three women instantly. Aya was crouched by the bulldozer, tightly attached to a little bar next to one of the wheels with a strange pair of leopard-print handcuffs. It was still chilly, but her whole face had gone red. Noah felt constantly self-conscious about his physique, since it was pored over and criticized on gossip sites, and he couldn't help noticing that the years had been exceedingly good to Aya. She looked embarrassed but indisputably hot.

Emi, sipping coffee with one hand on the bulldozer, was grinning. She'd had a tough time in high school, but Noah had heard all the gossip about her medical school accomplishments and her time as chief resident. He wasn't surprised that she radiated confidence.

The other woman was either Twyla or Martha. Back in the day, Noah had always been able to tell them apart, but it had been a long time since he'd seen either of them.

He often stuttered on names, anyway, so he found something else to say. Best to start with a vowel. He needed to sound authoritative, and getting tripped up over a consonant wouldn't accomplish that.

"I hope you're planning to leave by the time the work gets started," he said. "We're on a very tight timeline here, so we have to move things along."

"There won't be a festival," said Aya, staring up at him.

Emi suppressed a laugh. The other woman whipped out a notepad and began writing. Noah realized she must be Twyla, not Martha. He vaguely remembered hearing that Twyla had left a job at some major newspaper in order to come home and write for *The Love Hollow Post*. Noah never read his hometown newspaper, as all the articles about arrests and minor tragedies were just as depressing as the national news. But if Twyla had gotten up early in the morning to try to get a story on the little confrontation, she must really love her job.

He had to shut it down.

"The festival will be starting really s-soon," he said, coughing a little bit to try to disguise his stutter. "We've gotten all the permits that are required. Our crews have been hard at work."

Aya glared. "Permits are one thing. You didn't even think of asking for permission from the Zion Creek Memorial Museum."

Her tone was biting as she used the full name of the

place, and Noah looked away. Technically, Aya was wrong. Noah had thought of it, and Grace Kim, his PR manager, had recommended that they take that step. She had been very forceful, in fact. So Noah had told her it was fine. He said he knew everyone on the board of the museum as well as the director and had gotten their blessing.

Only parts of that were true. And if Grace came out to the site in the next few minutes, she would know for sure that they had a potential public-relations disaster on their hands. It would be terrible for not only the festival but also for Noah. Grace usually kept a cool head, so when she got angry, it was terrifying.

"Look," he said, holding up his hands. "I'm sure we can work something out."

"Yes," said Emi. "Thank God. Can we go convince Mama and Baba Chang to open early? I'm starving."

Twyla smiled, still taking notes. "They won't do it for you, Emi," she said. "You left us, remember? They'll do it for me."

Noah's stomach rumbled. He was flooded with memories of the Changs making baozi and savory pancakes for him on weekends. Noah hadn't even been a member of Emi and Aya's little club, though he hung around Aya enough to have some sort of honorary status. The Changs' restaurant was the first place outside his home where his skill with chopsticks was looked on with pride, not mockery.

Though Noah ate Chinese food all the time in LA, somehow, it wasn't the same. He had to use the private dining rooms to avoid being recognized, which tended to mean he was stuck with only the most expensive restaurants. Otherwise, he had to get takeout. It wasn't like eating at Chang's, with its faded calendars and spotless lazy Susans.

Aya was the holdout. She looked beautiful, sitting in the

dirt next to the bulldozer, her long hair braided back. She was wearing jeans and a college hoodie. He admired her choice of the UC Santa Cruz Banana Slugs, one of the zaniest mascots. She had at least two advanced degrees, including a doctorate, but she probably wouldn't wear any sweatshirts from those institutions. It wasn't like Aya to brag. She had probably always been too smart for him, and she was definitely too gorgeous for him too.

Noah forced himself to stop staring. "So, let's meet later, okay? At my office. We can work this all out," he said, addressing the group.

"No," said Aya firmly.

Noah was instinctively annoyed. If she had any idea the amount of work he had put into the event, the amount of time, the tiny details that seemed to take days to work out... But she was a typical academic, just sitting there, expecting her idealism to get things done.

"Deal," said Emi, whipping her hand out of the zip tie and standing up. "More coffee, Twyla. There's a good girl."

Twyla squinted at her. "I don't really have to listen to you, Emi. You're not that much older than me."

"But I'll always be older than you. That's the point," said Emi. "I'm that thing. I forget what it's called. Kouhai?"

"Senpai," said Aya and Noah at the same time. Their eyes met, and they looked away.

"The rock needs to stay," said Aya quickly.

Noah shook his head, hoping his voice sounded firm. "We'll talk about it. I'm sure my assistant—"

"We'll come by your parents' house later, Noah," said Emi. She took some nail clippers out of her pocket, snipped Aya free of her zip tie, and gave him a jaunty wave. "See you then!"

3

Aya The Love Hollow historic downtown was made for tourists, though they usually only had an influx in the summer months, and in recent years, that tide had slowed to a trickle. The streets were full of historic buildings, and after the mall had closed, some of the storefronts had been rehabilitated. Throughout that time, the Changs had kept their restaurant going, and they had always lived in the two-bedroom upstairs. One of the problems with their relatively small apartment was a lack of kitchen space, so they used the restaurant for all their personal cooking.

That virtually guaranteed that anyone who dropped in would get to eat amazing food. Twyla led them right in the back door, and Mama Chang fussed over all of them.

"Only three of you," she said. "Not eight! You won't be lucky."

Twyla gave a wry grin. "Emi is lucky, I guess? Right?"

Mama Chang understood immediately. "Ah, Emi! Yes, you did get married, you lucky girl. But you married so quickly! What? You didn't want your friends to be brides-maids? Why the rush? No shotgun wedding. I can see that. You're too skinny."

Emi gave a tight smile. "It was an efficient wedding. I didn't have that much time between finishing residency and starting work."

"Enough time to get married," said Mama Chang.

Twyla, ever the reporter, gave her a curious look. "I'm sure there's more to that story, Emi."

"If there is," said Emi a little sharply, "I don't plan on sharing it."

Mama Chang only smiled, shaking her head as she walked back to the kitchen.

Twyla sat back, looking stung. She might be a reporter, but Aya knew that Emi had always been gentle with her. Aya looked between them for a moment.

"Emi," she said slowly. "Why did you come back?"

For the first time, Aya realized that Emi was in a very tender moment. She was a newlywed. Yet almost as soon as she returned from her brief honeymoon, Emi had come back to Love Hollow alone. *Why isn't she with Charles, cherishing the rare moments of time they might spend together?*

"I came for you," insisted Emi. "What are you still doing here, Aya? My education took forever, but it's over now. What happened to yours?"

Aya was silent for a minute. "We're only twenty-eight," she said. "Lots of people finish doctorates in their forties."

"You're not lots of people," said Twyla. "*Xiexie*, Mama Chang!"

The women gave a chorus of thank-yous as a scallion pancake appeared on the table. It had arrived so quickly that either Baba Chang had made it while Mama Chang interrogated the newlywed, or they were simply serving up the food intended for their own breakfast. But Aya knew it would be useless to protest.

The pancake was quickly followed by three bowls of tomato-and-egg-noodle soup. Aya, Emi, and Twyla had been raised on Japanese and American cuisine, so they couldn't handle it when Mama Chang made dishes that were authentically spicy. They loved the blander Chinese staples, though.

"I don't have time to finish my doctorate," said Aya. "I'm running the museum singlehandedly."

Twyla hid her grin as she slurped noodles, but Aya noticed.

"You don't need to say anything," she snapped.

Twyla winked. "I get it! No comment. Speaking of which, do you think you could get that sizzling celebrity to agree to be interviewed on camera?"

"He doesn't do interviews on camera," said Aya. "He's self-conscious about his stutter. He'll let you record him but only if he trusts you not to use it."

"Wow, you sure do know a lot of details," said Emi. "Are you sure you haven't been in touch?"

"Everybody knows all that," snapped Aya. "It's all over social media."

Twyla and Emi gave each other a look.

"Oookay," said Twyla, putting down her chopsticks. She always ate quickly. Aya put it down to her status as a thin person. Twyla never ate slowly, took small bites, or pretended to have a delicate appetite. *Why would she?*

Aya, on the other hand, had learned that so-called "curves" were perilous in the real world. When she had dessert, it was in the privacy of her home. She only ate well with friends, not with colleagues, and definitely not on dates. In fact, a few years ago, she had deleted all of her dating apps, feeling a sick sense of satisfaction as the last one disappeared from her phone. *What's the point of giddy vulnerability anyway?* She had tried falling in love, and it had ended poorly. Besides, there was little point in aiming for marriage as some kind of end goal when it statistically would mean lots of stress and a shortened life expectancy for her. Only the constant successes she found in academia had been a balm for her brief foray into serious dating in high school. There was no dignity if you had to leave your study carrell and go scramble around, trying to make yourself attractive and uncomfortable.

"If Noah's not going to be interviewed, I at least need some sort of local interest puff piece," said Twyla.

"Why aren't they having you do the hard news?" Emi asked.

Twyla shrugged. "I was on sports before this. If I have to go to one more Rangers game, I can't answer for the consequences."

The Love Hollow Rangers were the high school football team, and Aya gave a weak smile at the thought. "If I got you on camera insulting the Rangers, *that* would be a local-interest story."

"Then I wouldn't have to quit my job. I'd be fired."

"Or killed," Emi agreed.

"So, an interview? An exclusive with the fabulous and gorgeously single Noah Kato?" asked Twyla, fluttering her eyes at Aya.

"Don't you have a conflict of interest?" asked Aya.

Twyla and Emi grinned at each other again.

"Not as much as you do. Tell me—are you going to wear something nice when you go meet your high school sweetheart?"

Aya shook her head. "No idea who you mean. As you

may recall, I was perennially single in high school. Oh, and what a coincidence! I still am."

Emi, the newlywed, had apparently turned into an old matchmaker as soon as she finished saying her vows. "You and Noah were perennially crushing on each other in high school," she said. "Weren't they, Twy?"

"It was disgusting," confirmed Twyla. "Way grosser than if you'd been in an actual relationship."

Aya finished her noodles. As dignified as she liked to seem, she never had any restraint around Mama Chang's cooking. Even in high school, when she was mortified by her appearance, gathering with her friends to make dumplings in the Changs' kitchen always made her feel better about it all.

"I need to get back to work," she said. "Twyla, find another interview subject. And Emi, stop grinning. It makes you look ridiculous. Come help me unpack the shirts for the Pilgrimage."

"Ooh, are you going to wear one later when you meet Noah?" shouted Twyla as they walked away.

Aya pretended not to hear.

4

Aya

As they were leaving, they came across a young family. A woman with a sleek brown bob was shepherding two boys and a husband, all in polo shirts, along Main Street.

"We should get Chinese," her husband said. "I'd love some egg foo young."

Emi smiled at the family. "They're closed today," she said.

The man stared at her. "All day?" he said.

Aya nodded. "Yes."

One of the boys scowled at them. "But you were just in there," he said.

Aya's eyes narrowed, but Emi interrupted. "Friends of the family," she said smoothly.

The other young boy pulled out his phone. "There's nothing to do in this town," he grumbled.

"Actually," said Emi, "if you're here for a bit, my friend runs the Zion Creek Memorial Museum. You should check it out. Closed at the moment, but it'll be open tomorrow."

"Is it in Zion Creek, though?" asked the woman, looking into the Changs' restaurant as if she didn't believe Emi's assertion. "Is that far from here?"

That gave Aya the opportunity to launch into her pitch. She hated doing a hard sell to random tourists, but with everything that had happened in the town, she had to get the word out about the museum.

"This used to be a town called Zion Creek," she said. "After the war, the town decided that the name was too deeply tied to Japanese American internment. So they decided to rename and rebrand, basically. The name Love Hollow was born, and with it, lots of slogans and merchandise."

"Love Happens in Love Hollow," said the father a bit too cheerfully.

"Exactly," said Aya forcefully.

"What war?" asked the older of the two boys. He looked as if he were at least fifteen. Aya guessed they weren't from Idaho and wondered what history curriculum had failed them.

"Word War II," she said, trying to inject patience into her voice. "After the attack on Pearl Harbor, Japanese American families were considered a security threat. Over a hundred thousand people were forced to live in so-called 'relocation centers' like the one here in Zion Creek. In most cases, they lost everything. Their homes, their farms, their property."

"That's crazy," said the boy, looking up from his phone. "Then what happened?"

"They had to do the best they could after the war," said Aya. "Many moved away. A couple of families stayed in the area, as there was one particular farmer who offered them work so they would have some kind of compensation."

"Well, there was formal compensation," said the father

of the boys as his wife started steering the younger one toward the diner down the street. "The government provided compensation."

"Twenty thousand dollars per person, issued a few decades later," said Emi with a smile. "After a lot of the people were dead. Pretty cheap price for freedom, huh?"

The dad only shrugged, but his son pulled out his phone. Aya couldn't see if he was fact-checking or just getting back to social media.

"I don't think they'll come," muttered Aya. "Thanks for trying."

Emi shrugged. "I thought I could be diplomatic," she said. "I guess I still can't."

"Nope. Neither can I. And that's why I've ruined the museum."

"Don't say that," said Emi as they watched the family go into Dottie's Diner. They were probably relieved to be entering an establishment where they wouldn't have to encounter any more opinionated young women, even if it meant missing out on egg foo young. Aya hoped they hadn't driven paying customers away from the Changs.

"It's only the truth," said Aya, turning away. "But whatever. Let's go back to my mom's. I need to get a few things done before this crazy meeting."

Her grumbled response made Emi smile.

"Yes, crazy meeting Noah Kato after all these years, isn't it?"

"Emi," said Aya, "don't even start."

5

Aya

Aya convinced Twyla and Emi to drop her off in the driveway of Noah's parents' house. The last thing she needed was the two of them twittering around, trying to get her to react as they relived every moment of high school. It was one reason she wished she'd gotten married. Apparently, the only way to survive in a small town as a single person was to ignore the way everyone tended to yell at you about getting back together with your high school sweetheart.

"I'm over him," Aya muttered, shuffling her feet as she climbed the stairs to the Katos' home. "They should get over him too."

Standing on their porch, she shooed Twyla away. Twy drove off in her beater of a car but not before stopping to whisper something to Emi. Aya tried to reclaim some of her dignity, pretending not to watch as the car left the neighborhood. She didn't need an audience for the little reunion.

After high school, she'd felt the loss of the Kato family

almost as deeply as she felt the rift that had come between her and Noah. The two families had always been close, and her mother was a frequent visitor there. But every time Aya visited, she stayed away. She and Noah had been together often growing up, taking trips out to the Kato farm to visit the uncles who still lived there and fidgeting through Saturday Japanese lessons with Noah's grandmother. All of her friends from the Single Lady Dumpling Club knew what it was like to be one of the few non-white high schoolers in Love Hollow, but only Noah's family understood the trauma of internment—as well as the particular kind of madness that had led a group of four young people to stay near the site of the trauma rather than flee to other cities, hoping to escape racism, or back to California, the only home they had ever known.

The dry breeze reminded her of the times she had stood there in high school. On many days she'd just been waiting for Noah so they could spend time together, studying or watching movies. She loved Japanese horror flicks like the original *Ringu*. He was terrified of them, but they provided a good diversion from the pressures of school and, eventually, an excuse for the two of them to get extra cozy.

Then there was that last night, the one before graduation, when she had come over to his house only to leave his porch without speaking to him. *What more was there to say?* She would only have been humiliating herself if she had gone through with the conversation, so she had walked home in a rare summer storm.

Before she could lose her nerve, the door swung open.

"Come in! Come in!" said Mrs. Kato, smiling deeply. "It's cold out there."

"Aya!" said her husband, who was lying on his belly in the living room. The principal of the local high school, Dr.

Kato was a dignified man, someone who wore a suit even when he was just heading to the grocery store on a weekend. Aya quickly realized he was lying on his belly because there was a beautiful baby next to him, a dark-haired little girl who had clearly just learned to crawl. She burbled, and though Aya had never really longed for a child, she felt a pang of panic. *How on earth has Noah managed to keep his kid out of the press?* She was fairly sure he wasn't married, so maybe that was how things had stayed private. *Who's the mother?* She must be white. The little one had the same hapa look that Twyla and Martha had shown as babies. Aya had more ambiguous features. Because she had her father's eyes, she was often mistaken for Latina or South Asian.

Mrs. Kato shook her head. "Being a grandparent is everything they say it is, of course. But if she spits up on that carpet one more time, we're just going to have to move."

Mr. Kato maneuvered himself into a sitting position with some difficulty. "How's the doctorate going, Aya? Good old Pile High and Deep? I would never have finished mine if it wasn't for *okaasan* over here pushing me."

Aya smiled. It had been a long time since she'd heard a PhD referred to as a "Pile High and Deep"—of manure, presumably. It was the sort of joke academics made when they didn't take their work too seriously. Her thesis advisor never made jokes like that.

Mrs. Kato shook her head. "It would have been better if we'd waited to have children. But both of us working, two little ones, and having to drive to the farm every weekend to help? It was far too much."

"Yes, clearly, you're doing nothing now," said Aya, taking off her shoes. She hesitated, wondering if she could move closer to the baby but not knowing precisely what to do with it.

Dr. Kato's cheery expression faded. "I'm sure your mother told you about everything that happened just before you came back. What a mess."

Aya shook her head. "My mom didn't want to worry me, but I did hear a little about it after I took the position at the museum," she lied. She had heard almost everything. The whole town was a hotbed of gossip, and her heart went out to Mr. Kato. He was tougher than he looked, but surely a firestorm of controversy wasn't what he'd thought he'd be dealing with when he took the principal job.

Mrs. Kato's mouth was in a thin line. "I told him he should quit. I almost did. Said it every day, in fact. But if the two of us left, what then? So now we're in a pickle. Neither of us can retire, but going on as we have is awful, frankly."

"It's part of our duty," said Mr. Kato. "Part of what we're being paid for. We have to deal with every person we encounter. We can't simply pick and choose."

"Please don't say this is just because I want to be *picky*," said Mrs. Kato, but she caught herself. "I'm sorry, Aya. Noah is expecting you, but he went for a walk, and I'm not sure whether he's back."

It really wasn't like Noah to abandon his kid with his parents, going off for a walk and not returning. In big cities, it was more common to have kids a bit later, but twenty-eight wasn't exactly a crazily young age anywhere. *And where would the mom have gone to? Is she with Noah?*

With even more dread, Aya tried to force a smile. "Sure, that's fine. I can wait."

"Why don't you go find him," said Mrs. Kato, who was bringing toys down from a box on her mantel and handing them solemnly to the baby. "He won't be far away."

"Sure," said Aya, taking only two steps back to the entrance and slipping her shoes on. "Thank you."

As she closed the door, she could hear Mr. Kato scolding his wife for scaring her off with all their talk of the town drama. She gave a small smile. Clearly, Noah hadn't told them the real purpose of her visit. If they had any idea, that was the drama they most certainly would have focused on.

6

———————

Noah

The mountains behind Love Hollow were most beautiful in summer, and Noah had a perfect view from his perch next to the creek. If he could just sit there, bathing in the beauty of nature, he wouldn't mind meditatively watching the seasons pass. He longed to go up in the mountains and hike, forgetting about all the pressures that were converging on him.

Noah kept track of the time using his old-fashioned watch, the kind that had to be wound, and he kept it as a sort of talisman. The higher he went in the music world, the more he noticed that everyone around him had expensive watches. His hadn't been cheap, setting him back over thirty thousand yen on his first trip to Tokyo, but it wasn't nearly as expensive as some of the status symbols he saw other guys wearing on their wrists. And it helped him maintain his hipster image.

Of course, if things played out the way he was afraid they might, he wouldn't be able to sell it for much. He remembered some story he'd read about New Orleanian musicians pawning their instruments then buying them back. If his label kept refusing his ideas, his earnings wouldn't be high for long. Coming back to Love Hollow was supposed to ground him, to make him feel like it wouldn't be so terrible to get a "real" job if he had to. Instead, it had done the opposite. His parents had relatively good public school jobs, and even they had been struggling mightily. If they had just accepted help from him, they could both have quit. Then again, because of how Noah's career was going, it was probably good that they hadn't.

And apart from his parents, nobody else in Love Hollow seemed to get it. They saw him as rich because he'd had enough commercial success to get famous. They didn't see how much he had to pay—agents, security, all sorts of costs. And a lot of the costs didn't go away when he stopped bringing in money.

He knew he was late for the meeting, but he couldn't bring himself to go down to the house. The idea of Aya sitting there with his parents, the way she used to many years ago, was painful. And they were just going to have to battle out the festival thing, which was maddening. Aya of all people should understand what he was trying to do. She probably hadn't even voted the previous year when his brother, Nobu, was running for mayor and certainly never came to a single campaign event. Granted, neither had he, but he'd offered to make a donation—though he ultimately couldn't, since it counted as outsider money. He could have contributed if he'd lived in Love Hollow, but as a nonresident, he was barred.

His parents had hinted more than once that Aya was "still" single, but he couldn't believe that was true. Even if it was, she hated him, and apparently had never been quite as interested in him back in high school as he'd let himself believe.

No need to make that mistake twice.

According to his watch, he was ten minutes late, so he forced himself to his feet. A few years ago, he'd developed a technique to get himself to go to interviews. First, he counted to ten, then he started walking or driving. And he didn't stop until the damn thing was over.

Celebrity had taken him by surprise. He'd always expected it to be the one thing that could give him the recognition he'd craved in high school. Freed of his Love Hollow identity, he could be cool, even impressive. Instead, he shied away from the attention, which only seemed to make it worse. And starting a festival had come with way more hassles than he had ever expected. It was almost like when he was just starting out and learning how to deal with renting recording studios and borrowing thousands of dollars' worth of equipment. Now he had people to make those decisions for him, but since he was officially in charge of a festival in his hometown, most things seemed to fall to him.

Noah was still walking, but the path petered out as he got closer to the creek. He swore under his breath. Once upon a time, he would never have made that mistake, but he hadn't been home often enough lately to remember. He would have to go into the creek to get home the short way. Otherwise, he'd have to backtrack and somehow scramble down the dirtiest and rockiest part of the foothills behind his parents' backyard.

Well, no reason to stop walking. He made his way through the water. It was higher than the last summer he'd been there, but he couldn't remember when that was. With work being so crazy, he preferred that his family visit him in

LA. The result was that his parents visited, his siblings almost never came, and he rarely made it home.

He had almost convinced himself that his conversation with Aya could be just a conversation. After all, he met all kinds of people through work, and many of them were so self-absorbed they could hardly be bothered to look up, let alone learn his name. At least that wasn't true of Aya. Though she didn't seem to respect anything he had achieved, at least she wasn't a fellow celeb.

Noah's feet stopped. When he started to take another step, he realized he was sinking in the mud next to the creek. The hiking boots he had worn seemed perfect, and they were certainly very expensive, but even they were not a match for the mud that was nearly up to his knees.

"Mom?" he called. "Dad? Hello!"

But there was no answer.

7

Aya recognized every part of the path. When she didn't find Noah, she knew he had gone down to the creek. The view was beautiful, after all. And that meant he must have taken the alternate route, the path that led from the road and formed the border of the Katos' backyard.

A bridge there always made people think of something very Japanese and traditional. Aya had never really been sure about it, as her vision of "Japanese" was heavily influenced by her family and the Katos. As a child, back when phone books were still a useful item, she had gone to San Francisco with her parents. She remembered the pages full of Japanese names. You could find a common name, like Kaneda, and simply follow it down the page.

In Love Hollow, Japan was represented by her family, Noah's family, Emi's family, and to some extent, by Sheena's dad before he left. That was it.

But when she arrived at the bridge, she found Noah next to it. He had gotten to the place on the other path where it spit everyone out in the creek and had apparently decided to go through the creek. He was standing there, looking a bit out of place. Clearly, Noah was no longer getting clothes that were loose on his slender frame. Both his jeans and his plaid shirt looked bespoke, ridiculously fancy for an afternoon in the Idaho wilderness.

"Hi," she said.

He nodded. "Long time no see."

They had seen each other that morning. But it must have been all he could come up with.

Aya and Noah both started talking at once, and she found herself deferring to him. "Sorry. You can go first."

He put a hand on his neck. "So, the festival is about to start. It's too late to move anything."

She raised her eyebrows. "*Move* the festival? Is that what you thought I wanted?"

He crossed his arms, looking a little bit wobbly. "I mean, that would have made sense a year ago. But now it's too late."

"Well, you should have asked me a year ago, then."

He glared at her. "You should have rrraised any objections a year ago."

The way he drew out the *r* sound reminded her of the old Noah, and if she hadn't been so angry about the point he was trying to make, she might have felt a little nostalgic.

In fact, it was a good thing that he was apparently now a jerk.

"Okay," she said. "If you're going to blame the victim, fine. First off, I thought it might not actually happen. You know, there are always stories in the news about festivals that don't work out."

"I'm sorry. Festivals s-s-spearheaded by *me* that don't work out?"

Noah had only stuttered because he was indignant but speaking softly. At some point as a teenager, he had learned that if he yelled in anger, he almost never stuttered. That worked pretty well until he got a reputation as an angry guy who always yelled, and he was forced to tone it down.

"Festivals period," she said, hoping she sounded calm. "Second, I thought you would at least have the decency to keep the main stage away from the museum during the one week of the year that we actually bring in revenue."

All the details of the Zion Creek Pilgrimage were already threatening to overwhelm her. The museum had held the event annually since it opened, and seeing people who were there as internees and their descendants never failed to move her. For her grandparents, it had been a hugely important event, a chance for them both to reconnect with old friends and to take pride as they showed off a successful farm and a growing extended family. Noah had once known how central it was, but apparently, holding a festival that would make the whole desert stink of weed was more important to him.

"The museum almost never brings in revenue?" he asked, and she kicked herself mentally.

"We do. I mean, that's not the point. That's not what being a nonprofit is about."

"If revenue is the main thing here... Listen, I can tell you—"

"It's not," snapped Aya. "The point is that you cannot allow this festival to go on right in the backyard of the camp. And to call it 'Love Hollow Lovefest' without even considering our history?"

She could see him exhaling. "I'm sorry. I'm getting a history lesson from you now?"

"I have a PhD in history!" she shouted at him. "Almost. I'm finishing it next semester."

The weight of the lie fell between them. Aya wondered, for a moment, if Noah was going to call her out on it. But what he said next was even uglier.

"Sue me," he said.

Aya's voice fell by half an octave. "Ex*cuse* me?"

"It's something I learned in the music industry. I'm going to do what I planned to, and if you have a big-enough problem with it, you and the museum will bring a lawsuit. And I'll deal with that lawsuit."

They definitely didn't have the budget for anything legal at all. Even as Aya thought through the people she could call who might offer something pro bono, it all seemed ridiculous. There wasn't time for a lawsuit anyway. The Pilgrimage was about to happen. So was the festival. Even if they could create some kind of legal trouble, it would never work in time.

In a sense, Noah was right. And that was what infuriated her. She hadn't dealt with the festival before, mostly because she hadn't wanted to talk to him, and now it was too late to do anything.

"I'm not going to sue you," she said. "And I don't know if I can stop the festival." She leaned on the side of the bridge. "But fuck you, Noah Kato. I will do every single thing I can, and I will go down trying to stop it."

She walked away, listening to his plea.

"Aya, please. You can't just leave."

"I certainly can," she said without turning.

"You really can't. I'm stuck."

8

Noah

Aya hesitated. She was probably wondering if she could just walk over the next hill and call the fire department.

"Please," he said again. "If the fire department comes to rescue me, it's going to be all over the news."

"All publicity is good publicity," she said, turning to look at him.

"Yes, but it would be humiliating," he said, aware that he was begging. "And I'm sure they have better things to do."

Aya took a step closer to him. "If I pull you out, you'll cancel the festival?"

"I'll make some concessions. I'll write up a formal proposal, not just to you but to your whole board."

He felt shocked that he had used the word "proposal" with her. But she didn't seem to notice. She was contemplating the offer.

"Fine," she said. "We'll read what you have to offer."

He felt so weak with relief that he almost fell over and sank into the creek.

"There's a red box at the base of the bridge," he said. "It's sort of built into the third step? It looks like it's locked, but it's actually not. You'll see that."

Aya walked over then called out to him when she found it, "What am I supposed to do with this? I take it you don't need a tourniquet."

"No. B-B-But you should use that harness just to make sure you don't fall."

She came back wearing the harness, its rope with carabiners thrown over her shoulder, and she went to the top of the bridge. Standing there in the creek, he had another chance to see just how beautiful Aya had become over the years. Though he didn't visit often, Aya's mom seemed to "drop by" the house each time he was around. Every time she pulled out her phone, with its photo of her three daughters, he avoided looking directly at them as if he might go blind. Back in high school, Aya had been obsessed with straightening her hair, and she wore it in a fashionable ponytail with a sort of stripe on the side. But now she was wearing it loose. With her silky hair blowing in the breeze, Aya looked like a goddess who had suddenly decided to wear jeans and a quilted jacket. And with the harness around her, she was also his savior.

"Okay," Noah said. "Just clip it around one of the posts on the bridge. If you get on your belly, you should be able to reach me."

If he had been several inches closer, he would have been able to pull himself up to the bridge. But he was just far enough that he knew it would be a stupid move. Though Aya was short, he'd be able to reach her arm without a problem.

"Fine," she said, and he could see that she had turned a

little bit pink. "So now what? You're just going to grab my hand?"

She got on her stomach, stretching out an arm to him.

"I'm going to grab your arm here," he said, getting a tight hold next to her elbow. "And you grab mine."

He looked up at her, and for a moment, he was distracted. Her eyes were earnest and kind. Aya was concentrating, showing a different emotion from the tidal wave of resentment he had felt just a moment ago.

"On the count of three," he said, trying to remember exactly how to do it, "I'm going to try to jump up and grab the bridge. So just stay as steady as you can. One, two, three."

It was a scramble, and it wasn't easy, but Aya was steadier than he'd thought. He caught hold of the part of the bridge that had been just beyond his reach and dragged himself up. When he got purchase with his feet, he had to awkwardly straddle the railing then let himself down. He ended up next to Aya, his jeans so muddy that it looked almost as if they ended at his knees.

Aya laughed. "What a mess! I would have had no idea how to do that if you hadn't told me."

He raised his eyebrows. "Yeah, well, I have some experience."

"I guess so," she said. "Given that your family apparently keeps all the equipment for exactly this sort of rescue maneuver in the bridge. Who got stuck here last time? Your mom?"

He frowned. "Why would you assume it was my mom?"

Her good humor still hadn't dissipated. "Oh, she hated when we got too near the creek without 'proper supervision,' remember? I always thought it was because she didn't like it back here."

He smiled dreamily, thinking of one afternoon when Aya had come over and they had tried panning for gold. It was probably because of that riveting lesson on the gold rush in third grade. They had ended up filthy, and Noah had been grounded, though Mrs. Kato didn't do anything to Aya beyond giving her a stern lecture about playing in creeks without an adult. Aya was a guest, so no matter what her behavior was, it was not going to be harshly punished.

"No," he said, sighing. "It wasn't my mom. But anyway, it doesn't matter. I mean, thanks."

She saw through his answer immediately. "It was you, wasn't it? Wow, Noah. Did you lose your boots that time too?"

He gave a mournful look at the muddy spot where his beautiful boots had disappeared, possibly forever. "No, I was just wearing some...um, slides."

Aya was laughing still, rocking back and forth, her whole body heaving as she made fun of him. With anyone else, Noah would have gotten annoyed, but she looked so beautiful that he couldn't really get angry.

Until she regained her composure, took the harness off, and handed it to him.

"So. I hope I can expect your formal document today? I'll present it to the board. Your parents seem pretty busy with the, um, the grandbaby, so I know they have better things to do than sit through a lot of emergency meetings."

Noah looked away. "I mean, they don't get a vote anymore, do they? Not after what happened, you know."

Aya was furious. "They should never have resigned. You're right. They don't vote. But the meetings are public, so they always attend."

She had looked irritated before, but now her eyes were

flashing, fury in her voice as she stood up and stomped down the bridge.

"Aya, thanks," he said. "And yeah, I'll have my assistant send the p-proposal in."

He hadn't meant to step in it again, but he could tell it was the wrong thing to say.

Aya laughed again but with bitterness. "Oh, excellent. I'll have my own imaginary assistant read the proposal, draft a response, convene a meeting, do the million other things that need to happen before the Pilgrimage, and maybe have dinner with my mom and sisters too. Or maybe your assistant can take care of that while he's at it."

"She," said Noah weakly. "Her name is Grace."

"Excellent," snapped Aya. "I look forward to doing business with *Grace*."

And with that, she was gone.

9

Noah

"I have a c-confession to make," Noah said to Grace the next morning. It was time he came clean with his assistant. She was going to wonder about the document he was asking her to send to Aya.

Unless he didn't send them. Aya's sarcastic comments about her lack of help were still ringing in Noah's ears.

"That's nice," said Grace. "And I have a problem for you. A rather large one, as it happens."

He looked up instantly. They were in the space downtown that they were using as a makeshift office. It looked great on the surface, a series of unoccupied rooms in what used to be an elementary school. But Noah had quickly realized it was a magnet for autograph seekers, so he and Grace had made friends with one of the managers and always dashed in and out of a side door. It was only a matter of time until that became public knowledge, too, and Noah would be stuck spending hours signing copies of his first album—the one where he had a ridiculous Mohawk—for people he couldn't remember.

Grace was used to solving problems. So when she came to Noah with something, it usually meant it was something rather large.

"Booker Cadence passed on Ella's next album."

Noah tilted his head, inhaling. Though he had never been the best Japanese language student in the Kato family, he found himself using it to respond whenever he didn't know what to say and didn't want to stutter. It was perfect, as it expressed some sort of reaction without committing him to anything.

"I h-heard that album," he said. "It's not a huge surprise that they passed."

"No, but it does mean that Ella's about ready to jump ship."

Ella Chang, one of the daughters of the couple who owned Love Hollow's only Chinese restaurant, was the other kid who had "made it" in the music industry. She'd gone to Nashville as soon as she graduated, eventually following Noah out to California and to his label. Booker Cadence Records had money, reputation, and a great deal of experience. Things had worked out for Ella for a long time.

But like Noah, she had begun to chafe against the limitations that Booker Cadence put on her. They were particularly harsh with the female stars, ruthlessly regulating both their appearance and their politics. Noah, as a skinny man, didn't tend to get a lot of lectures from them about how he looked, though they liked him to starve himself before every photo shoot so that his muscles would look better. But Ella heard about pretty much everything she wore in public and even the outfits she put on just to leave the house.

"Does she want to be part of the festival too?"

Grace looked at him with pity. "She was the first one you asked, remember? And she said she didn't want to do it."

He nodded. "Something about not wanting her parents to get caught up in all of it?"

Grace nodded. "Yes. There will probably be a couple of pieces about their restaurant, but if she's not performing, business will be great for a week, and the customers will get more attention than the chefs."

Noah went over to the window. An elderly woman across the street seemed to be installing at least five wind chimes on her porch. The cacophony was interesting, and he wondered if he could use it in one of his songs. Of course, it would have to be a more avant-garde piece of music than Booker Cadence would allow him to make, so he didn't mention it to Grace.

"Ella's successful," said Grace. "She's brilliant at self-promotion, better than any team she's ever hired. And she's ready to shop this album around."

"I can't help," said Noah shortly. "She knows what the bosses want, and if she's not doing it, that's her choice."

"Yes, but what label will she go to?" asked Grace. "Nothing quite meets her needs, especially if she doesn't want to move. She needs a creative partner."

Noah got the same feeling that he always did when his mom asked him to come to yet another baptism or mass—guilt combined with a nearly crazy desire not to do what was being asked of him.

"I can't help her, Grace," he said. "But I'll talk to her. How's that?"

"Fine. Now, what were you going to talk to me about?"

"Nothing," he mumbled. "There were some issues with the local Japanese internment museum, but my family cofounded that place. I can handle it."

"Sounds like a good thing for me to do," said Grace briskly. "You always get weird when it comes to your family."

"No," he insisted. "I can take care of it. And if it gets worse, I'll let you know."

She gave him a mock salute. "Fine. Because the last thing we need at this point is bad publicity. If everything goes perfectly, we'll manage to break even but only just."

"So much for music festivals being a great way to get rich, huh?"

Grace shook her head. "I don't know why you thought that. I really don't. Nobody would have made the mistake of saying something like that to you."

Noah pulled over his computer, wondering how he was supposed to draft the kind of document he had never even attempted to write. "Well, it may not make me rich. But that was never the point anyway."

He started writing.

10

———

Aya

Aya got the document from Noah as an email attachment. It felt strange to think that Noah Kato was just out there, writing emails. Then again, it had probably come from one of his minions. He'd seemed very surprised earlier that he might even consider doing some work himself. Apparently, after you make your millions in the music industry, you never work again.

Aya had read the celebrity gossip, though she pretended not to. Noah had been prolific at first, releasing at least one album every year as he climbed the charts. But the last few years had been full of slowdowns, and there were rumors that his label might drop him. He was a star, but that label specialized in megastars, and apparently, there was no room for error.

She rolled her eyes as she skimmed his stupid document. The proposal was not nearly good enough. It seemed they weren't going to move the festival at all, although they could shift the main entrance to the site they were going to use as a secondary entrance. During the ceremonial part of the Zion Creek Pilgrimage, the second evening, the festival could try to do a longer break between sets, but that wouldn't really keep people quiet. Worst of all, they were keeping the main stage exactly where it was, right at the edge of the museum's land. The landscape was going to look ridiculous. Plus, there wouldn't be a single reference to Zion Creek and its sad history.

"What an idiot," she murmured, reading through it. "He really thinks he's doing something."

"Is this Noah?" asked Emi. She'd been on her knees, sorting through boxes of shirts to try to make sure they had enough extra-small long-sleeved ones for the elders. "What does he think he's doing?"

Aya chose to ignore her tone. "He thinks he's making improvements, but he's just shifting around deck chairs on the *Titanic*."

That made Emi laugh. "Oh, so his festival is going to sink, is it? Seems unsinkable to me."

"The Pilgrimage is unsinkable," muttered Aya. "Or it should be."

Emi was rubbing one of the shirts, but she had stopped sorting. She didn't respond.

"Emi?"

Rubbing her face, Emi said, "I'm sorry. I just got tired all of a sudden."

Aya grabbed the box. "It's fine."

It wasn't fine, in fact. If Emi could tolerate the grueling schedule of medical school and residency, she should be able to sort a few T-shirts. She had once cared a lot about the Pilgrimage, too, though she hadn't been back very often since high school. Aya and Emi had both sworn they would never live in Love Hollow again, but Emi was the only one who had actually stayed away.

"So," said Emi. "That thing Mama Chang said about my wedding."

She looked so miserable that Aya shoved the box aside.

"She shouldn't have said that, okay? She still thinks of us as her twins' surrogate big sisters. But it's just noise. You really don't have to listen."

"That's kind of disrespectful," said Emi, frowning. "And the thing is—"

"No," said Aya. "You don't get to do this. Seriously, you have no idea what it's like, facing Mama Chang and everyone else."

Emi shook her head. "That's not what I—"

Aya didn't usually interrupt, but she felt absolutely crushed under the mountain of tasks she had to complete. It was only the third Pilgrimage she had managed, but she'd made the questionable decision to expand registration in order to bring in revenue, and she was quickly understanding why previous events had been capped at three hundred. This year's crowd was unmanageable, but she had to succeed. So she found herself talking over Emi, and once she had started speaking, her speech ran away with her.

"I have been dealing with meddlesome, supposedly well-meaning people gossiping about my unmarried state for years, okay? I'm sure they did it when I was gone, but living here is a million times worse. And I love Mama Chang, but she's one of the worst offenders. Yes, I'm sure I would hear something if I were married, but just someone talking about how I should have had more bridesmaids? It would be completely different."

"Sorry," said Emi, but Aya could tell she had more to say. And Aya barreled over her.

"You've done the thing that society wants you to do, okay? You aced med school, you were chief resident, you found a man who is both intelligent and hot, and you had a super-quick wedding with essentially zero drama. Do you know how it feels to have literally none of that? Do you have any idea?"

Emi held up her hands. "Slow down."

"No," said Aya.

"I don't even know what we're fighting about," said Emi slowly, "but I can tell that I've really touched a nerve."

The old Emi would have been angrier, but the new Emi was talking as if she were lifting quotes directly from some pamphlet about dealing with difficult people. She'd probably had experience talking down patients with schizophrenia, and that annoyed Aya even more.

"You know," she said, "you're right. This isn't your fault. It's Noah's."

And before Emi could stop her, Aya left.

11

Noah

Aya was chaining her bike to the same rack they had used as elementary school kids. She had biked to school more often than he had, as her family lived closer. But Noah had done it once or twice, mainly because he didn't want to be left out. Aya was faster than he was, but he tried hard to keep up. Even as a kid, he'd always had the sense that he couldn't measure up to Aya. She was smarter and funnier than he was, and he always had the sense that she'd go far. Celebrity was supposed to insulate him from that feeling, but instead, it had made it worse. Not only was Aya close to getting a prestigious doctorate, but she'd also spent years of her life propping up a museum that his parents adored. She would be able to point to a way that she'd made her mark on the world, whereas all he had to show for his last decade of life were some albums that already sounded dated.

Aya saw Noah watching her and glared. She didn't wave.

"Dammit," he said. As usual, he didn't stutter on the word, but he did succeed in getting Grace's attention.

"What is it?"

"Just a crazy townie," Noah said, wincing as he lied. "I'd better go head her off."

"She won't be able to get in," said Grace without looking up from her computer. "Ever since I made Mike send that memo, nobody is buzzing in random strangers."

Noah shook his head. Grace really needed to learn more about small-town life. Aya was sure to chat with someone, figure out that they had a cousin or friend in common, and find her way in. Love Hollow was big enough that not everyone knew one another but small enough that you were somehow connected to just about everybody.

And sure enough, Aya was soon knocking on his office door.

"Hi," said Noah. His voice was artificially cheerful. "How are you doing, Aya?"

"Not so well," she said. She was unfolding something from the pocket of her jeans. He tried not to look too hard at the jeans. Her cheeks were flushed from the bike ride, and she looked just as beautiful as she had the day before. Normally, Grace gave him a hard time about his penchant for hanging out with beautiful women and never making a move. Sometimes, those women made the first move themselves, of course, and that was always the end of their friendship. But Grace probably wasn't going to comment on how gorgeous Aya was. Aya's anger was even more noteworthy than her flushed cheeks or her beautiful hazel eyes.

"I don't know what you thought you were doing with this proposal," Aya said. "But I'm not bringing it to the board. There's no way this will help mitigate the damage you're doing to our event."

"What's..." But Noah couldn't get the next word out.

Which was unfortunate because Aya thought she knew what he was going to say.

"What's the harm in one bad event? Funny you should ask, Noah. We might have to shut down the museum, as it happens. Bet you didn't think plain, old-fashioned lack of money would spell our doom rather than all of that shit your parents went through, but that's the reality."

Noah tried not to feel happy that she had used his name, but he failed. He realized he would rather have Aya rant at him than hear praise from pretty much any other human being.

Grace cautiously stepped into the fray. "Noah's parents are objectively wonderful," she said.

As usual, Grace's instincts had been good, and Aya softened for a moment. "They've done everything they could," she said. "But it might still amount to nothing if we have to close our doors."

Grace gave a solemn nod. "Well, we can't let that happen. Let me see what I can do."

Aya was still hesitant. She smoothed the piece of paper. "I was under the impression that this proposal *was* the best you could do."

Grace gave a wide smile, as if it were Christmas morning and she were presenting the room with home-baked cinnamon rolls. "Well, if it doesn't work for you, we will absolutely have to find something that does."

"Yes," said Noah, and Aya instantly snapped from doubtful to angry.

"No," Aya said. "You can work on it or not. I don't care. But I think my original plan was a good one, and I'll be sure that more press than just Twyla covers this story."

"One more chance," said Grace. "We'll bring you something better, and we'll get this off your plate."

Aya looked skeptical, but at least Grace's assurances got her to leave.

But as soon as Aya was out the door, Grace turned slowly to him. "I don't know why you didn't bring this to me. I already told you this festival cannot afford negative publicity now."

"I didn't want to bother you with it."

"Well," she said, a hard edge of sarcasm in her voice, "now it looks like I've put my name on an event that will be a failure. And my reputation is on the line, because anyone who finds out about the bad PR for this festival is going to associate it with me. They will be especially surprised that we're fighting with an Asian American history museum. And since most people won't figure out that Grace Kim is a Korean name, they'll think it's some kind of internalized racism bullshit. Or just gross incompetence."

Noah couldn't argue with her. She was right.

"W-What do I need to do to make it right?" he asked.

"You can't," she snapped. "But you can leave those for me," she said, pointing at the papers. "And you can leave."

He couldn't ever remember having an argument with Grace that couldn't be talked out. Or one with Aya, for that matter, until that night in high school.

"Are you sure?"

"Noah. Just. Go."

12

—————

Aya

It took Aya some time to connect with Emi again, which was unusual. Her texts went unanswered for hours. But she didn't have time to waste with actual phone calls. She spent the whole afternoon trying to get the museum in decent shape for all the guests who were about to descend. Though real estate prices in Love Hollow were relatively low, Aya felt like she would never be able to afford a house. But if she ever bought one, she'd probably make a pretty good homeowner. A lot of what she dealt with at work seemed to fall into the home ec category. The septic system was unreliable, every fresh paint job seemed to look scuffed and worn after a mere six months, and random repairs that the internet hadn't prepared her to handle popped up regularly. Because they were trying to save on cleaning, that fell to Aya as well, so the bathrooms in particular needed to be deep cleaned. She didn't manage to fix the dryers, but she did put the paper towels she'd ordered in rather attractive piles, and she added fresh flowers to her list of things to buy.

Emi didn't arrive at the museum until it was almost time for dinner, and Aya tried to keep from scolding her.

"Everything okay?" she asked, and Emi nodded quite vigorously.

"Absolutely. I just needed a walk. It's supposed to rain later, so I took advantage of the weather."

Aya wished she could have taken advantage of the weather rather than be stuck inside, though she didn't say it. The morning had actually been beautiful, and her bike ride to the elementary school had contained scenic vistas that would likely make the tourists drool in a week's time, but she hadn't been able to enjoy any of them. She led Emi over to the all-purpose room, where she had taken out some of the leftovers from an exhibit they had done on local maps.

"Any news on the music festival front?" asked Emi, looking over a topographical map of the surrounding area. "Did you get a chance to speak to Noah?"

Aya shook her head. "I spoke to his assistant, which was definitely more useful. She's clearly the brains behind the festival."

"Aya," said Emi, "Noah's smart."

"Well, not about these things. Grace seemed really great."

"So what's she going to do?" asked Emi, looking around the all-purpose room for a chair. Not finding one, she sat with her legs under her on one section of the floor with a small amount of carpet. Aya, who had always hated *seza*, traditional Japanese seating, sat cross-legged beside her. "I don't know. She didn't specify."

"But you think she'll do more than Noah was offering? She'll move that one stage you hated?"

Though there wasn't any doubt in Emi's voice, Aya started to feel angry again. "Grace didn't commit to anything," she said. "She probably won't do anything! I just fell for her whole act because she was responsive. She has better manners than Noah."

Emi shrugged. "I didn't mean to imply anything like that, Aya. She might be great. Who knows?"

"No," said Aya, standing again. "If this is going to work out, this has to be an actual battle. And I'm going to need help from everyone who's going on this Pilgrimage."

"Are you sure that's wise?" Emi was still seated, looking like she was about to do a tea ceremony, not go to war. "At this point, none of the Pilgrimage guests even know, right?"

Aya shook her head. "They're absolutely going to know when we try to do the opening ceremony and there's a whole screaming crowd right behind them, stinking of cheap beer."

That only made Emi smile. "I'm sure some of the beer will be really good, actually. I heard they have partnerships with microbreweries."

Aya couldn't laugh. "I have an idea. Are you coming or not?"

Emi stood. "Actually, I was thinking about heading back to your mom's place. I'm feeling kind of tired."

"Well," said Aya, "I'm going to need a photographer."

13

Noah

When Noah tired of his cold war with Grace, he went home early. His dad worked summers, but his mom was off, and she was crawling around on the floor after little Hana again.

"Where's Nami?" he asked. "Wasn't she off work today?"

His mother nodded. "I insisted on taking Hana for a few hours, though. Give Nami a little time to herself."

Noah, exhausted from his workday, shrugged. "Doesn't Nami have a lot of days off in the summer?"

His mother gave him a pitying look. Hana was chewing on a little toy monkey, gurgling.

"Hardly off, dear. She has a baby."

"Yes, time off to spend with the baby." Noah had been gone when Hana was born, which was probably for the best. Every time he saw Nami, he had trouble understanding her choices. A lot of their conversations seemed to focus on how poorly she was sleeping at night or how hard it was to get anything done during the day. He always wondered why she had a baby if she found it so tiring.

"You know I don't say this lightly, Noah," said his mother, and he rolled his eyes.

"Let me guess. If I ever have a ch-child, I'll understand."

"Close," she said, her tone clipped. "My son, I have tried my hardest to raise you with feminist ideals. But the truth is unless you become a woman then have a child then deal with all the crushing expectations surrounding all of that, you may come close to understanding. Until then, forget it."

He would have responded, but his dad chose that moment to come home. "You are a saint, dear," he said to his wife, kissing the top of her head. He was carrying two large canvas bags, which he put on the kitchen table. "Dinner is served, but we'll start without you if you'd prefer."

"Yes," she said, "I will lie down for just a moment. Noah would say it's unreasonable, as apparently my adoration for this baby is supposed to make me some sort of fountain of youth, but I'm exhausted."

"Mom," he complained, but she put a hand on his arm.

"Worn to a raveling," she said as she patted Hana on the back. The quote was from one of the Beatrix Potter stories she used to read him and a peace offering. She blew him a kiss as she headed off to her bedroom.

"F-Fine," he muttered. "Dad, what is this?"

He was looking through the bags, finding all sorts of glass containers full of food.

His father put away his suit jacket, added his tie to the hanger, and nestled Hana into her high chair. The thing looked like a piece of expensive modernist furniture, the type of thing that Noah would buy in LA then come to quickly hate.

"We started doing this with the Changs a while ago," he said. "Nami said hot food in plastic is bad for you, and it saves them a bit of money."

Hana started banging on her tray, and her grandfather kissed her before passing her some little cup contraption. Hana sucked down the milk then banged the new toy on her tray.

"I'm in trouble with mom," confessed Noah.

His father chuckled. "Of course you are. You haven't given Nobu your answer yet."

Noah frowned. "What do you mean?"

"His engagement party," said his dad, carefully mixing a bit of soup into some rice before spooning it into Hana's mouth. The baby stared at him.

"Does he want me to sing?" asked Noah.

There was silence for a moment. "No, son. He wants to know if you're going."

"Okay. I mean, some people are interested in my music."

Noah's dad expertly used a mere corner of a napkin to get some stray grains of rice off the baby's chin. "Yes. Well, that part, I can't speak to. Are you going to the party?"

"Of course I'm going to the party," Noah grumbled. "I don't know why Nobu is even asking. Or why he's asking you."

"Most likely because you did not RSVP," said Mr. Kato, ever the diplomat. He had inherited the Japanese ability to argue politely.

"Okay, well, it's not like I would miss it," said Noah.

His dad smiled. "Well, you miss things sometimes. You're busy. He and Hunter simply wanted to know."

Noah pulled out his phone. "I'm going to text him now," he said.

"Plus one?"

"No," Noah said. "Just me. I mean, I could ask Grace."

"Grace has already been invited," said a voice, and

Noah's mother appeared around the corner. "She RSVP'd right away, of course."

"Yeah, yeah, she does everything better than me."

"Except sing, perhaps?" said Noah's dad. "Or is she an expert in that too?"

"Apparently not," said Noah's mother without waiting for him to answer. "And it's a good thing, too, or she would put our son out of a job."

Noah served himself some of the Changs' soup. His mother and father, without speaking, switched places, and his mother began feeding baby Hana.

"In some ways, it might be fun to try another job," said Noah lightly. He didn't want his parents to worry about the very real possibility that his career was going down the tubes, but he imagined they had seen the same celebrity gossip everyone else had.

"You could take care of Hana for a day," said Noah's mother, a wicked smile on her face. "Generally, all it takes to root out a bit of deep-seated misogyny is a nice long chunk of time during which one is solely responsible for a helpless baby."

"Now, dear," said Noah's dad, patting his wife's hand. "Hana is far from helpless. If she were helpless, we couldn't leave her with her uncle."

"Of course not," said the proud grandmother, making a shocked face at the baby, who giggled.

"I don't need to be a nanny to take care of her," said Noah. "And I don't think I have too much misogyny that needs rooting out. Thanks, Mom."

His parents exchanged looks, and his father nodded.

"Well, then. There's a reading-intervention training Nami wanted to do. It's after the festival, so maybe you could take one of those days. Your mother and I were going to split them."

Noah shrugged. "Sure. Whatever."

14

Aya

"So, about your doctorate," said Emi.

"You just want me to get one so I can have a couple of letters in front of my name," grumbled Aya. "Here, stand with the museum in the background and look wistful."

"I'm not even signed up to attend the Pilgrimage," said Emi. "Not officially."

"Stand still," said Aya. She had borrowed one of Twyla's old cameras. She always thought it was a shame that Twy had decided to report news, not simply take pictures. Then again, she was forced to do so much at the local paper that her articles often included a picture she'd taken herself.

Emi tried again. "I wouldn't want you to go out and get a doctorate if you hadn't already done most of the work," she said. "But something has kept you in that program for seven years."

"Eight years, actually," said Aya through gritted teeth. "Though only six before I took this job."

Emi shook her head. "Sure, however many years. I know at one point you liked it. So what changed?"

When Aya didn't answer right away, Emi gave her a sly smile. "Actually, I could ask that same question about Noah. You liked him, so what changed?"

"You know what happened back then," said Aya right away, but Emi only shook her head.

"You never talked about it, remember?"

Aya gritted her teeth. "Okay, well, let me give you the short version. First, I talked to Nobu. Sit over there, okay? I think that gets us the best angle of this stupid stage."

Emi walked over to the spot Aya had indicated. She was moving slowly, probably because she was trying to process new information about an event that had happened a very long time ago.

"I can see why talking to Nobu might have put you off," said Emi slowly.

Aya glared. "What? Because he's gay?"

"No! Because he was a jerk in high school."

"He still is, for all I know," said Aya. "We haven't talked in years. Luckily, it's not that hard to avoid him."

But Emi was shaking her head. "He really isn't, Aya. He hasn't been, not for a long time."

Aya looked out over the deserted festival site. She wanted to say that people didn't change, but she'd never believed that. She was certainly a different person from the shy young girl who couldn't hide fast enough at every high school dance. Senior prom had been the only exception, thanks to Noah, and look how *that* had turned out.

"Well," said Aya, "it doesn't matter. Back then, he was a jerk, but he still knew things. And he let me know that Noah wasn't really interested in dating."

"Oh, come on," said Emi. "Noah was all over you."

The long summer day was fading quickly behind banks of clouds, and Aya felt a raindrop on her hand. She tried to shield the camera. The pictures of Emi were going to look very dramatic, but Twy would be furious if she got the camera wet.

"He was interested in dancing with me," Aya corrected her. "Flirting, maybe. But what I imagined, actually dating? That wasn't going to happen."

"Because you didn't let it happen," said Emi.

Aya didn't speak. There was more to the story, and Emi was one of her few friends who had been there through the whole thing. But she wasn't ready to share it.

"I think we should go in," said Emi. "The storm is only going to get worse."

The rain was steady, and Emi's suggestion was very reasonable. But Aya looked at the landscape, which took her mind off those high school memories. Emi looked forlorn, a darkly devastated speck on the bare land, and Aya took as many pictures as she could.

"Stay there for a moment," she said. "We're finally getting something."

By the time they left, Aya was satisfied. At least she had ammunition. She and Emi had both gotten soaked, but she'd managed to shield the camera, and at least some of the pictures were going to be great.

She just had to find it within herself to take Noah down.

15

———————

Aya

"Physician, heal thyself," said Aya as Emi stretched out on the couch.

It was the wrong joke. Aya was sitting at her mother's kitchen table, using her laptop to try to make sure they had finalized the right type of accommodations for a guest who was in a wheelchair. Only two hotels in town had rooms that were not only accessible but also convenient, and the Love Hollow College vacant dorm rooms they had rented out for the rest of the crew were not going to work. Aya had to pray that nobody had made a mistake and booked out one of those rooms she'd reserved at the Valley Inn and Suites, but when she'd called earlier, the receptionist hadn't seemed sure about the whole thing. If she had found a minute to go over there, she could probably have worked it out, but she had been too busy dealing with the festival—the same festival that was behind all those hotel reservations. If they had taken that room to give to some stupid "celebrity" singer, Aya would have to find a way around it.

Aya's mom had always panicked when her children were

sick. She had one hand on Emi's back. As soon as she'd come home from the dance studio, she'd rushed over, shocked to find her houseguest ill.

Aya, on the other hand, hadn't even bothered with a hot shower when they'd come in, soaked to the skin. She'd gone right back to work, but somehow, Emi was the one who had gotten sick.

"Aya, can you put on some water for tea?" asked her mother. There was a note of reprimand in her voice. Japanese American mothers did not let wet children come into their home without rushing them into a hot bath, and tea was almost as essential.

Emi spoke. "Is there an Urgent Care-type place in Love Hollow these days? No, right?"

Her voice sounded terrible. Aya looked up. "Can't you just go to bed and sleep it off?"

"This level of... shortness of breath could be dangerous," said Emi. "It could be a PE."

Aya's face must have been blank. She could tell her mom didn't know the term either.

"Pulmonary embolism," said Emi. "In other words, serious."

She was leaning over, her head practically on her knees, and Aya blinked. "Pulmonary embolism? What are we supposed to do for that?"

"In the city, I would say ambulance," said Emi. "But we're so close to the hospital. Maybe you could just drive me."

Aya's mother drove them both. She was worried, her hands shaking as she parked right at the entrance. Aya walked in with her friend. Emi was rushed right back as soon as they arrived at the Love Hollow United Hospital emergency room, which made Aya feel even worse. She held

Emi's arm throughout the triage process. Emi had to shake her off in order to get her blood pressure taken, and the nurse tutted at the numbers.

"It's a little high, probably because I'm stressed," said Emi.

The nurse nodded. "Well, let's get you into a room."

It must have been the wrong thing to say. Aya thought Emi looked a little paler. And after they were shown to a room, Emi leaned back on the hospital bed.

"What's going to happen now?" Aya asked as soon as the nurse had left. It seemed like nobody was explaining anything to her, but she didn't want to ask. Everyone seemed to agree with Emi that she might be having a so-called "PE," and that was sending Aya into a doom spiral. "They can do something soon, right?"

It appeared her questions were still not going to be answered.

"Aya," said Emi. "I love you. But your panic right now? It's not helping."

Aya's face fell. "I'm sorry," she said. "I hate hospitals."

Emi's breathing was ragged, but she squeezed Aya's hand. She had been right by Aya's side as Aya's dad suffered through cancer treatment, a harsh and devastating regime that hadn't ended up working. She understood.

"I know hospitals," she managed. "So go to the cafeteria, and don't come back until you've gotten some work done."

"Work? I can't work."

"Pilgrimage," said Emi, and she coughed. "Don't you have more hotel rooms to fix?"

Aya did have various things she could have fixed. But she had brought only her phone, not a computer, so she found herself in the hospital cafeteria half an hour later, staring at a piece of pumpkin pie. It put her in mind of

Thanksgiving. She hadn't been thankful for much of anything lately, she realized. Whatever the opposite of gratitude was seemed to have taken over her life, so much so that she had been sent away from the bedside of her best friend.

Emi had said she wanted to text Charles herself, so Aya didn't even have that task to distract her. She flicked through different national news sites, feeling progressively worse with each one. But without something else to read, she didn't know what she would do.

"Hey," said Noah. "What's going on?"

Aya almost jumped out of her seat. He was there, wearing black pants and a mauve jacket that must have been borrowed from his brother, concern etched across his face. "Has the doctor seen Emi yet?"

"No," said Aya. "Though I guess she's seen herself."

He smiled. "It's still so weird to think of her as a doctor. It's like she went on that trip to China then came back with this crazy obsession with knocking out life milestones all at once."

Out of loyalty, Aya didn't say anything, but she had noticed the same thing. When Emi came back from China, she'd definitely seemed depressed. But shortly after, she started looking at property, married Charles, and decided to spend her last days of freedom volunteering for the Pilgrimage.

"She's worried it might be a lung problem," said Aya. "How did you know she was here anyway?"

He shrugged. "I could just say Love Hollow, but it's actually more than that. I owed Twyla a phone call, and she said you guys were here. So now I owe her a favor too."

Aya touched her pie with a fork and caught Noah looking at her.

"Do you want to talk about some new terms now that

we're both here?" he asked. "Honestly, I really think we can make it work. I just need a little more time."

She recoiled. Talking with Noah had been such a relief, so peaceful, that it had lulled her into believing they were back in high school. They used to sit together at lunch every day, sneaking off to eat in different parts of the building. She knew there were rumors that they did more than eat bento boxes together, but there was nothing to those rumors. Just being in the same room as Noah had been a balm to her soul and also so electrifying that she could hardly think straight.

"I only want to deal with Grace," she said abruptly.

He shook his head. "Aya, why not me? Couldn't we just have a conversation?"

"No," she said shortly, and she pushed the pie to one side. "Look, I don't know what I'm going to do about this festival. But just thinking about it is making me angry. The one strategy I had was this amateur photoshoot in the rain, and it seems like I almost killed my best friend trying to get a good angle."

"That sounds like something Chen would do," said Noah, but his grin faded as he saw that Aya was crying.

"Look," he said, reaching for her hand. "We don't have to talk about it. I promise. But can I stay?"

"Sure," she said, too shocked to remove her hand from his grip. Eventually, she had to, daubing at her tears with her sleeve.

Noah got up then returned with napkins. "One minute," he said. He came back with two steaming Styrofoam cups of tea, a carton of milk, and three sugar packets.

"I did rinse your tea bag," he said. "But since it's the second brew, it's not going to have as much caffeine. So let me know if you want another cup after this."

She gave him a grateful smile. Since most of the people she'd grown up with were not Japanese, the custom she'd learned from her family of "rinsing" the tea leaves before steeping them in hot water was considered strange. One of her pet peeves was paying a hefty sum of money for a cup of tea with old leaves that hadn't been rinsed. She tended to drink coffee for that reason but figured that Noah had probably made the right call in avoiding the hospital coffee.

"Why did you bring a carton of milk?" she asked. "Are you on a calcium kick?"

He shook his head. "Low-quality tea," he said, apologetically. "It's chai too. Plenty of milk and sugar will make it slightly better. Good thing you have pie."

She instantly felt her lack of manners. "I'm so sorry," she said. "Do you want some?"

He shook his head. "I'm on a cleanse. There's a photo shoot in a month. The label guys wouldn't even want me to put sugar in my tea, actually."

Aya looked disbelieving. "And you're staying with your family right now, even though you're on this cleanse thing?"

He gave her a smile, but it looked sad. "Yeah, Dad can't stand to see me diet. Mom objects on principle, but as long as I'm cooking, she's less pushy about what I eat."

Aya smiled. She'd always remembered that about the Kato family. Though the grandparents and parents took on most of the cooking on weekends, each child had been responsible for one weekday meal from a fairly young age. Noah had always cooked on Tuesdays, generally chicken curry rice, his favorite. Aya, whose mother never let her do anything in the kitchen, always found the arrangement rather shocking.

She found herself unable to eat her pie. As it turned out,

sitting with someone who was on a work-mandated diet killed her appetite.

"Aya," said Noah, and she snapped back to herself.

"Hmm?"

"You didn't kill your best friend," he said, "or almost kill her."

She took a sip of the tea, willing herself to calm down. "I was the one who got her out in the rain," she said. "If not for that, she wouldn't even be here."

"Typically, healthy young people don't have severe lung problems after getting a little wet during a storm," he said. "I'm not a doctor, but even I know that."

"Well, she was fine before," snapped Aya. "So obviously I didn't intend for this to happen, but you're not talking me out of what I saw."

Her phone began to buzz.

"I have to go," she told him.

She didn't turn around to see whether he would finish her slice of pie, but as soon as she left, she wished she had taken it with her.

16

Noah

Noah saw Twyla as he was leaving the hospital. He wanted to stay but decided he wasn't going to do any good sitting in the cafeteria. Maybe he could get into his makeshift studio and record a few ideas. He always tried to do that when he was waiting for something to happen.

Twyla was sitting in her car in the parking lot. He could hear her music playing, as her windows were down. She liked country but only old-school country, and she loved to sing along. Her singing was terribly off-key, but thanks to all her dancing, she had a fantastic sense of rhythm. The song she was singing along to was some old ballad about driving back home at midnight, and Noah couldn't help noticing it was a fairly accurate description of his situation—except the heartbreak, of course. Noah just sang about having a broken heart. He wouldn't know what that was like in real life.

"Thank you," he said.

She nodded. "Of course. For what?"

"For letting me know about Emi. I don't know what's going on with her, but I think they let Aya back in."

Twyla grinned. "Emi's fine. That con artist, she's convincing them to discharge her tonight. She probably sweet-talked Dr. Flores. Guess if you spend enough time in hospitals, you learn how to pull some strings, right?"

Noah could ask around and probably get an answer as to what was wrong with Emi, but if it wasn't public knowledge, he would try to refrain from asking. Twyla would have been more specific if Emi wanted people to know. Ever since the tabloids had tried to get warm and cozy with Noah's personal life, getting a little too close to a truth that would have shocked their readership, he had tried to err on the side of respecting others.

"Well, thanks," he said. "I owe you one."

"An interview?" asked Twyla. "Well, what a coincidence. Because I could really use a good interview. Consider this me calling in the favor."

"I don't really d-do interviews these days," said Noah, and as he stuttered, he was reminded why. "But if you need festival tickets, let me know."

Twyla laughed. "I have a press badge, dude. Tickets are the last thing I would need."

He nodded. "Well, yeah. Anything else, just let me know."

Twyla's face lit up. "Oh! Come to think of it, there is something."

Her grin was so wide that Noah dreaded the explanation. "Okay, great. What is it?"

As Twyla described what she wanted him to do, Noah felt some serious reservations. But Aya was pushing Emi's wheelchair through the doors of the hospital. In a bigger city, they would have insisted that a nurse escort the patient to her car, but in Love Hollow, a trusted local could get around some of the regulations. Emi, who was grinning, almost jumped out of the chair. The two of them headed over, arm in arm, and Noah was out of time. If he wanted to avoid speaking with them, he was going to have to leave. Giving them a little wave, he nodded to Twyla.

"I'll make it happen," he said. "But I can't promise I'll be very good."

"Oh, Noah," she said, "I'm sure you'll be good enough."

17

———————

Aya

"Oof, my back," said Twyla.

Twyla was lounging on the couch, reading the news on her phone, having demolished two slices of quiche and a large bowl of miso soup. Aya rolled her eyes at her sister, who did not look up. Twy's back did not appear to be injured.

"Want me to take a look?" Emi asked then took a sip of coffee.

Twyla looked up, smiling. "Nah. It's nothing a doctor can cure. I have a very specific problem."

"Bye, Twy," said Aya, heading for the door.

"Are you sure I can't come with you?" asked Emi. "I don't know what you think I'm going to do all day."

"Wait for Charles," said Twyla. "Ooh, the first flight out! It's so romantic."

"Actually, I convinced him not to get that flight."

"Do tell," the reporter said, looking up hungrily.

Aya, who was waiting to leave, sighed as she waited for Emi to tell the story. If Charles wasn't coming, she might need to stay with Emi, in spite of all the things she needed to get done.

"He has a big work thing tomorrow," said Emi. "So we're going to wait until that's over, then I'll fly back and join him."

"Is that safe?" asked Aya and Twyla at the same time.

Aya gave her sister a grudging smile.

"Yes," said Emi firmly. "Nobody needs to baby me. I'm pregnant, not in an iron lung."

Aya shook her head. "I can't believe it. You don't look pregnant at all."

"Well, I'm sure I look tired, which is pretty much the par for the course during the first trimester," said Emi. "But after last night, I'm just glad not to be dying."

"We're all dying," said Aya automatically.

Emi rolled her eyes. "Yes. Indeed. Thank you for the reminder."

"Stay and rest," said Aya, but as soon as she touched the door, Twyla started complaining about her back again.

"My back feels so very terrible! It will only feel better if my dear sister and her friend come to the dance rehearsal tonight!"

In a hushed voice, she added, "Emi, you don't have to come. Better play that pregnancy card for the whole nine months."

Emi smiled. "I'll come, but I don't think I can do any of the moves. In spite of your mom's best efforts, I was never much of a dancer."

"Same," said Aya, but Twyla held up a finger. "You're showing up to help us make the numbers, Aya-nene."

Using Aya's childhood nickname was manipulative, and it almost worked.

"Mom can lead and follow, and come to think of it, so

can you," said Aya. "So you never have any issues with numbers."

"Yes, but we have too many leaders now. We need three followers, so Mom and I can't fix it by ourselves, and it's going to be so sad if one of our best dancers doesn't participate," said Twyla. "Promise you'll come?"

Aya groaned. "Will you come with me and help me make welcome packets?"

"I would, but I have to get to work!" said Twyla, springing to her feet as she proved that her back problems were entirely imaginary.

Emi grinned. "Okay, crazy lady," she said. "I'll help you make the packets. Let's go."

18

Aya

Aya felt guilty that she hadn't been doing anything for her mother, sister, or friend—but not guilty enough to go to the rehearsal.

"We have to get moving," said her mother as soon as everyone had finished eating. "It's okay if you don't come, sweet Aya mine. I know you've been busy."

Her mother used to say that kind of thing all the time, down to the silly nickname. After their dad died, Aya, Martha, and Twyla had been basically the most doted-on children in existence. Their mother and grandmothers felt like they needed love more than discipline. Fortunately, Auntie Joan often came by to take care of them after school, and since she had never really liked kids, she was much stricter. The combination of high expectations and boundless love helped them recover.

"Aya," said Twyla, "you need to come with us. Or Emi is going to feel much worse."

Emi got up, glaring at Twyla. "I feel just fine, thanks."

"Okay, so you're going to join in the dancing?"

Emi grabbed Aya's hand. "Actually, I take it back. I feel terrible. I could faint at any moment."

Aya wore a silky green dress that Twyla had given her. She recognized it from one of the recitals her mom's students had done about twelve years ago. She was surprised at how well it fit but embarrassed by how short the skirt was and how deep it plunged down her back.

"Can't I just wear street clothes?" she asked Twyla.

"Not if everyone else is wearing their costumes," said Emi, grinning.

"Why should I wear this? They wore long skirts to these dances! It doesn't make any sense."

"But this is a modern take," said Twyla. "Old-school dance with a little bit of fresh, youthful energy."

"I don't have any energy at all," grumbled Aya.

"Ooh, Aya-nene," said Twyla. "When you dance, you'll get your energy back."

It was a maddening thing to say, but Twyla was right. When they arrived at the studio, Aya felt some of her stress dissipating as soon as she smelled the familiar scent. It was a combination of polish, sweat, and the faint aroma of energy bars. Everyone complained about the lack of designated parking, but the building her mother had rented in the historic downtown area was a beautiful one. And it was so ancient that the rent stayed low. It would probably have been hard to get anyone besides a dance studio to use the space. At night, most people just used the parking lot next to the bank down the block.

Aya's mom had a warm-up routine that still made Aya laugh every time she did it. It was always obvious that she had come of age as a dancer in the eighties, as the Jazzercise moves owed a great deal to the kind of singers who paired tight leotards with huge hairstyles. And she quickly noticed that only some of the dancers were wearing costumes.

As soon as they got started on the actual choreography, Twyla left the room, returning with the one and only Noah Kato.

Everyone in the room gave a collective gasp. Love Hollow might be very proud of their famous Noah, but that didn't mean they got to see a lot of him. Since the group was made up of a combination of community volunteers and the high school seniors in the Hanson Dance Troupe, some of the folks in the room had never met Noah at all.

"Okay, okay," said Aya's mom, smiling and gesturing at everyone to quiet down. "Since Mr. and Dr. Flores couldn't make it tonight, we needed one more couple to take their place. And I am *very* proud of having taught Noah Kato some of these swing dance moves myself!"

The audience gave a little round of applause.

"We need a follower," she said. "Aya, *kinasai.*"

Aya didn't move. "Twy knows it," she said weakly.

Twyla was already standing off to the side with an older gentleman, grinning as she shook her head. "I'm already in the dance. But the two of you can stand in for the Flores family. Then we won't be off."

Aya was still shaking her head. "I don't know the moves," she said.

"It'll stop you from back leading," said her mother smoothly. "The followers don't need to know the dance. I gave Noah the practice video. Okay, everyone! Places."

Aya felt like it was a middle school dance. She wanted to stay far from Noah, and she didn't usually find swing dance particularly exciting, but somehow, even the standard Lindy hop position made her feel both thrilled and unspeakably awkward. His hand was on her waist, her right hand in his left.

He shifted but smiled. "So you still back lead. Is that right?"

She frowned. "Only if the leader needs help," she said. "I consider it a favor to them."

"Well, I need a lot of help," he said. "So take it away, Hanson."

She couldn't help laughing just as the music began, which almost made her miss the beginning. She was expecting a slow ballad, maybe even perhaps the ironically titled "Don't Fence Me In" that played in the background of pretty much every single documentary about Japanese American internment. But her mom never liked that for their demonstrations, reminding everyone that everyday emotions like love and jealousy were always at play on the dance floor. "My parents are proof," she always said. "I wasn't born nine months after one of those dances, but my older sister was!"

Always burning with ambition for her students, Aya's mother had gone and chosen an insane song for their dance. "Don't Sit Under the Apple Tree" was just about as fast as those songs could get.

Aya started breathing quickly. If Emi had been the dancer, with her new pregnancy breathing problems, she would probably have passed out, so it was just as well that she was sitting on the side. Aya quickly abandoned the triple steps that she liked to do while swing dancing. There simply wasn't time. Even if she did the bare minimum with her feet for every move, she still risked falling behind.

Noah grinned. "Not bad, huh?" he asked.

Aya stared up at him, her eyes wide. After the next turn,

she shook her head. "Where did you learn to dance like this?"

"From your mom, remember? I did a bunch of demos. And I signed up for lessons in LA at the same studio as one of the owners of Booker Cadence. Ultimately, that's why they signed me."

There were a few more turns, so she couldn't answer. When they got to the move where he spun her out and she kicked her way around him, she could talk again. "Why doesn't everyone try to get a record deal that way?"

He smirked, which wasn't much like the Noah she remembered. "Others tried. But it was a tough studio. They only let you into the advanced group if you were really good."

And Noah was good.

19

A^{ya} "Beautiful!" said Aya's mom.

The group clapped, and somebody whistled. A suspicion began to dawn on Aya, but because she was a little embarrassed, she talked to Noah about it first.

"Do you really think Mr. and Dr. Flores end the whole thing with a huge solo?"

She wasn't sure how old the couple would be, but they at least had grandchildren. Mr. Flores owned a trucking company, and Dr. Flores was a respected OB-GYN at the local hospital. Presumably, she'd had to work. *But why would her husband have skipped the rehearsal?* Usually, as the owner of a small business, Mr. Flores would be fairly free so late in the evening.

One of the other older dancers raised her eyebrows at Noah. "Well done, young man," she said.

Noah nodded, grinning. "Th-Thank you."

Aya realized he wasn't embarrassed by the praise. The old Noah always hated hanging around after their performances. Once, he had bought her a carnation, but as soon as he gave it to her, he ran off. They both should have stayed after the Love Hollow Unplugged event, the alternative they'd organized to the boring school-wide "Talent Show," but she had ended up soaking in the praise without Noah. He really couldn't stand people telling him what a wonderful job he had done, and having to suppress his stutter in every interaction usually took away the high of the show.

But now he was accepting the praise as if he'd expected it and adding in words of thanks.

"So glad I didn't miss it. Great to be d-dancing in this studio again."

He was working the crowd. And Aya couldn't help but find it sexy.

"Oh my *god*, you were amazing," said a familiar voice, and Aya shrank. A tall, skinny blonde was loping over to them, staring at Noah. "Noah Kato, what the hell are you doing here?"

He bowed out with a smile, turning to a pair of older ladies who were asking after his mother. Aya realized the new part of Noah must also be a result of his time in show business. He was able to get out of the attention more gracefully than he ever had.

Carson Cobb, the blonde, had always been thin. Back in high school, she gave lots of details on how many inches she needed to lose off her already-tiny waist in order to get the kind of modeling contracts she wanted. When she'd gotten married to J. P. Wilmer, son of one of the richest and most influential Love Hollow families, her wedding was the biggest the town had ever seen. It seemed like everyone in town was either working the event or attending as a guest.

Carson had even appeared on a reality TV show, "Something Blue for I Do," which seemed to be all about ways to spend insane amounts of money on something that was going to be worn once. In Carson's case, Aya recalled, it had been a sapphire toe ring.

Carson's smile fell away when she turned to Aya. "So," she said. "I heard this was the last time you all were doing that old-people event."

Aya felt a chill. "No. We do them every year. As you probably know."

Carson had lived in Love Hollow her whole life, but perhaps she ignored the crowds. And as part-owner of one of the largest hotels in town, she really should have known more about local events.

"I thought this was the last one," she said. "But maybe I heard wrong."

"Yes. We'd be happy to use your hotel for some of the bookings. Next year, that is. There wasn't anything available this year."

Carson grinned. "Oh yes. We're all booked up with the festival. Noah is doing wonderful things for this town, aren't you?"

Noah had returned, and Carson gave him a dazzling smile. She hung on his arm, praising him, and all Aya could think about was how young she looked. She was only four years older than they were, but she almost looked like she could have been a teenager. Her skin was perfect, her makeup expertly done, and the wrap she was wearing over her dance clothes made her look like she was modeling for a line of dance clothing. Which was strange, in a way. *Why is it necessary to sit in the wings, dressed for dance, to pick up a cousin who almost certainly has her own car?*

She was saved from any additional reflections as Emi and Twyla came up to the group.

"Carson Leary," said Emi, leaning in for a hug. "Tell me how you've been! It's been years."

"But it's Carson Wilmer now, right?" asked Twyla. "So hard to keep track of everyone's names these days."

"Oh, it's Carson Leary," said the blonde, folding her arms.

Twyla snapped her fingers. "That's right! The divorce. See? I told you it was hard to keep track of names in this town, Emi."

Aya gave a small wave to the group and melted away toward the parking lot. She thought that the board had been doing a pretty good job of keeping the museum's funding situation private, but if someone as far removed as Carson had heard rumors that they would have to close, that wasn't a good sign. It made her shudder to think of closing up everything and letting music festivals and hiking trails beat down the only relics of the war era the town had left.

Noah was on her heels. "Hey," he said. "Sorry about that. Fans can be a little pushy at times, you know? You get used to it."

"Carson's always been pushy," Aya said, wiping her eyes. "It's not that."

"Hey. What's going on?"

"Just thinking about those old dances," she lied. "You know, that was all Jiji would ever to say to me about the camp. That he got to dance with lots of beautiful girls, like Baba. And she would laugh and pretend to scold him. He never told me more, because he wanted to shield everyone, you know?"

His face fell. "They talked about it together," he said.

"Your grandparents and my grandparents. Not when they thought we were listening, but they did."

He hugged Aya, the force of her grief and the thrill of the embrace taking her breath away. She kept her head buried in his shoulder, the soft fabric of his shirt letting her hide her face. As soon as she raised her head, she was conscious again of where they were standing—just a small dark bank parking lot, where students and volunteers were making their way to their cars, quietly heading back to their homes for an unexceptional weeknight.

She swallowed. "Thanks," she said.

"I don't suppose this means you'll go easy on Grace?"

It was a misstep, and he must have noticed that as soon as he said it.

"Noah," she said. "This is what I've been trying to explain to you the whole time. The space that our grandparents had, to talk, to remember? That's what's at stake here. And I'm not going to give that up just because your name is on this festival."

"But seriously," he said. "The way I see it is this..."

She held up a hand. All the feelings that had been flaring up for him were lost under the weight of his denial. "Forget it," she said. "I'll deal with Grace. But I hoped that, just for one moment, you would understand."

It would have been great to drive off herself in that moment, to get into some fast car and take off, tires squealing. But she had to go back to the studio to find Emi and Twyla. It was unclear whether she was saving them from Carson or she was saving Carson from them. Poor Emma, Carson's young cousin, probably wanted to leave. The two couldn't be more different in personality, and Aya had heard from Emma's mother that they didn't get along. All the more suspicious for Carson to show up tonight.

By the time Aya came back out, Noah was gone, and she suppressed her disappointment.

"Twyla, that was interesting, but you know the Flores family needs to get back in there, right? I'm not doing that again."

"Okay," said Twyla, and there was a hint of doubt in her voice. But Aya chose not to hear it.

20

———————

Aya

"Mrs. Irving called," said Aya's mother. She was sitting at the end of Aya's bed, as she had when her daughters were little.

Aya blinked. As a graduate student, she'd gotten used to having her own schedule. Sure, she had to teach a class here and there, but most of her work involved research. Ever since coming home, though, she had been woken early. Twyla had become an obsessively early riser as a reporter, and she didn't think that her sister's night-owl nature needed to give way to her own drive to meet deadlines. And their mother was physically incapable of letting a morning go by without cooking breakfast for her daughters. So each morning, the sounds of water boiling, the kitchen fan running, and bacon sizzling all conspired to wake Aya up. She could have used earplugs, but she couldn't bear not to come down for breakfast when her mom was going to so much trouble to make it for her.

"Did you tell Mrs. Irving I didn't live here anymore?"

moaned Aya. "Please tell her I've left the state. Or the country."

Her mom smiled. "She'd find you, Aya. She doesn't miss a trick, as you know."

Aya did know. She supposed she should have been thankful that Mrs. Irving had taken over as president of the Zion Creek Memorial Museum board. She'd done absolutely everything she could to shore up the museum's finances, and without the grants she'd gotten, they already would have closed. Even the cost of heating the place through the winter would have proved overwhelming. But Mrs. Irving was an expert at alienating people, and they were not likely to get many local visitors back on their side when they had a tyrant at the helm.

"I guess I have to call a meeting," mumbled Aya. "I've failed at getting the festival in line. She's going to kill me."

"If she really killed people, Love Hollow would be empty," said her mother. Then she paused. "Aya, I'm sorry about the dress. At the time, I didn't think..."

Of course her mother felt the dress had been too skimpy, and after a couple of decades of constantly feeling she was too fat for nice clothes, Aya didn't want to hear it. She couldn't stand talking to her mother about fashion. Theirs had never been a home where she was allowed free rein to wear what she liked. If it didn't make her look good, it had to go. Aya remembered how red she had gotten the year her mom stopped letting her wear spaghetti-strap shirts. There was a green dress she had loved, but when she talked to her mom about her plan to walk back from Chang's with her friends, it had been forbidden. Apparently, it wasn't good enough for the people of Love Hollow to see.

"It's fine, Mom," she said. "Don't worry. I won't wear it again."

"Aya," she said, but Aya was already getting up and heading to the bathroom down the hall.

"I also don't need to be in the dance," she called back. "You should have Twy do it, then maybe Noah will agree to the interview."

Her mom said something else, but Aya didn't hear her. If she was going to face Mrs. Irving, she needed to shower, and she definitely needed at least one cup of coffee in her before she tackled that conversation.

21

Aya

When Aya came downstairs and looked at her phone, she found a missed call, but it wasn't from Mrs. Irving. It was from her thesis advisor, which was even scarier. Professor Jin only called when she had something serious to talk out.

"Good morning," Emi called out weakly. Then she looked at Twyla. "Does Aya know yet?"

"I know Mrs. Irving called," said Aya. "I guess she called Mom to get to me. But my advisor called too."

"Yeah," said Twyla. "Well, we probably know why Mrs. Irving called. Here's what seems to have happened—"

"I have to call the professor back," interrupted Aya. "When she calls, it's always about something important."

Twyla looked at Emi, who was frowning. "Um, you might want to read today's headlines first."

"We're not all obsessed with the news, like you are," said Aya, looking around for her hair tie. The problem about her mom's house was if she put something down, someone else might use it. And she felt an illogical impulse to look at least slightly dressed up for her mentor. It wouldn't do to come across as sloppy in front of Professor Jin. "Some of us are obsessed with things that happened many, many decades ago. If it's not on microfiche yet, I don't need to be bothered."

Emi grabbed Aya's phone. "You do need to be bothered with this, though."

Aya tried to take her phone back, but Twyla thrust her own phone in front of her.

"Aya. Seriously. You need to read these."

She snatched Twyla's phone then sank into her seat at the kitchen table.

A dark, grainy photograph showed her with Noah in the parking lot. It must have been taken just at the minute she pulled away. Neither face was perfectly visible, but plenty of her nearly naked back was. And from the angle the photograph was taken, it looked like a smoldering affair, not two friends pulling away from a platonic embrace.

Twyla smirked. "A picture is worth a thousand words," she said.

"Why didn't you tell me you kissed him?" asked Emi.

Aya frowned. "I didn't kiss him! I just gave him a hug."

Chuckling was their only response, so she kept defending herself.

"Seriously, that was it. Whoever took this probably has a bunch of others where it's obvious that we just had the world's quickest hug."

She tried not to blush as she said it. In fact, it had not been the world's quickest hug, not exactly.

"No surprise they chose to publish that one, then," said Twyla. "Want to call your mentor now?"

Aya would have much preferred to call her friend Sheena. What she needed was Sheena's frank, swear-ridden take on what was going on. But she also didn't think she could handle any more teasing about Noah, so she didn't make the call.

She was pretty sure nobody could have recognized her from that photo, but apparently, her name was already all over the internet. She was referred to as a "local dancer" more than once, which might have been funny if it didn't have definite "stripper" connotations. She hoped that showed that some sneaky non-local photographer snuck into the parking lot to take the picture. It was a little easier to hate a villain who was from out of town. Nobody in Love Hollow would ever have made that mistake.

Out on the porch, Aya took a deep breath to steady herself before she called her mentor.

"Nice celebrity boyfriend," said Professor Jin, answering on the first ring. "Mind telling me why you're off dancing with Noah Kato rather than sending me your next draft?"

"It wasn't for fun," said Aya. "That was work."

Professor Jin did not suffer fools gladly. "Well, Aya," she said, "I might remind you that your work is still paid for by this university."

"If they funded it better, I wouldn't have had to take the job at the museum," said Aya. She hated going against Professor Jin, but she had gotten a lot out of the protests she saw happening at other universities. Finally, it seemed, there was at least a little acceptance that it wasn't right for only people with trust funds to be able to live on graduate student salaries. That activism had not exactly spread to Eastern Rock University quite yet, but it might in the future.

"You will have to choose," said Professor Jin. "Or perhaps you already have. And, Aya, I do not think your choice is a wise one."

Aya stuck her lip out. This was much harder than

arguing with Emi. "I have time," she said. "There's no rule saying I have to finish the dissertation right away."

"Nor is there a rule saying you have to run that museum," said her mentor. "If the job is too much for you, it would be better to find one less demanding while you finish your work. I respect that you need employment, but surely being the sole employee of a very busy nonprofit is not ideal for a scholar."

"They weren't able to find anyone," said Aya. "Not with how the salary is. And the lack of benefits."

Professor Jin sighed. "I cannot tell you how to live," she said. "But with the archive you have at your fingertips, it would be a shame to throw away both your research and your training."

You are *telling me how to live, Professor,* thought Aya. *In fact, you always have.*

But she didn't say that. And she regretted speaking her mind, as her professor's next words chilled her.

"Be careful about the sort of attention you attract," she said. "The new leaders of our university are extremely conservative, and they have already talked about changes they would like to see. Do not give them any excuse to think you are not a serious scholar."

"I didn't ask to attract attention!" cried Aya. "I was helping my mom with a class, for my job, on a weeknight. Love Hollow is the most boring town on earth. I never thought it would become a national story."

"Well, you know how quickly narratives can take on a life of their own," said Professor Jin. "If nothing else, you should have learned at least that from your work."

Aya remained silent.

"Is there anything in it?" asked the professor.

"What?"

"I mean, this thing with Noah Kato. You're not going to give up your career for him, are you? Because he seems like someone who would not be able to make the accommodations needed for you to continue your work."

Aya clutched her phone. "There is *nothing* in it. There were rumors in high school."

Her professor was too smart to be put off by that. "Were the rumors true?"

Aya shook her head, though Professor Jin wouldn't be able to see it over the phone. "We went to prom together. That was *it*. Classic case of people thinking the two Japanese kids in the school needed to date each other."

Another silence followed. "Well, good. Have your next draft to me by the end of the holiday."

Only Professor Jin would expect one of her mentees to finish a dissertation draft over the Fourth of July weekend. The troubling thing was she must have been very serious. And her tone had been sterner than usual. If she dropped Aya, that might be it for the doctoral program.

And all at once, it felt just as awkward and twisted as that fateful night in high school.

Aya ended the call but was unable to head back into the house. Professor Jin's questioning had taken her straight back to prom night—otherwise known as the most beautiful, torturous night of her life.

22

———

Aya

When Aya and Noah arrived at prom, Aya's first stop was at the drinks table.

They weren't alcoholic, of course. But something about those star-spangled cups seemed to confer a little liquid courage anyway, as if the cheap, store-brand soda were begging her to come back to her senses, to remember that this was just the school gym dolled up in lots of confetti and strange posters.

But she had trouble remembering that. She'd always hated the music that was popular in high school, preferring instead old ballads and revolutionary folk music from the sixties and seventies. She didn't really know the nuances of anything that had happened during those decades, of course, but it sure sounded good on the guitar. The way her white classmates yelled the lyrics to all the rap music was jarring, and the pop music felt like something from an arcade game.

Aya had spent a great deal of time finding a dress. Her mother had suggested several they could have sent away for, but they were expensive. Eventually, Aya and her friends decided that wearing short dresses would give them many more options. Emi and Sheena were going with a large group of uncoupled people, and they were already enjoying themselves. Celine was with Leo, the exchange student she had been dating for a year, and they were already dancing. Aya had eventually settled on a fit-and-flare black dress with meticulously layered shapewear beneath it. She still felt like she looked a teensy bit fat, but it got her much closer to a body she would have liked than anything else she'd tried. And it showed enough cleavage that Sheena unhelpfully referred to it as the "Oh shit!" dress.

Noah went off to talk to some of their classmates. He didn't really like soda. Aya could see him with a group of girls, his head towering over theirs.

Nobu, who was volunteering at the drinks table, gave a long sigh. "My brother, right? He's always been such a favorite with the ladies."

Aya gave a tight smile. "Yeah, well, that's what happens when you do all the A-Wing stuff."

A-Wing was the place Aya and Noah spent most of their time. The school theater was there along with the rooms where the choir, band, and orchestra practiced. Both of them had been in the choir for ages, and Noah played trombone in the band as well as jazz band.

And most of the activities were more or less packed with girls. The guys at Love Hollow Senior High were much more likely to do sports or even overtly academic stuff like the math team rather than risk having to appear in a tuxedo with a bright-red bow tie. Noah, who genuinely loved music, was an exception.

"Aya," said Nobu. "I have to tell you something. College

is going to be a lot easier for you if you don't go there with a lot of expectations."

She turned and looked at him. Aya was first in the class, a shoo-in for valedictorian, and though she knew college would be harder, she didn't think she was likely to flunk out. Nobu was only in his first year, but the rumor mill was already running. Apparently, his performance was lackadaisical, and Dr. and Mrs. Kato were begging him to transfer rather than quit entirely.

"I can hack it," she said. It was the phrase she always used when she wasn't quite sure if she could achieve something.

"Sure," he said. "I mean, academically, you'll be fine. But don't expect any of this high school stuff to go with you to college. Best if you plan on being unattached. Know what I mean?"

Noah made his way over. "Dude, nice shirt," he said, laughing. The volunteers were supposed to wear all black, but Nobu's shirt had glow-in-the-dark stars on it.

The older brother stuck out his tongue. "Looks better than your tux," he said. "Good thing you won't be keeping that."

"C'mon, Aya," said Noah. "This music sucks. Let's go bother the DJ."

"Okay," said Aya, faking a smile. But the warning resonated in her head as she crossed the room with Noah.

Apparently, Noah wasn't taking their relationship as seriously as she had thought. And that was a good thing for her to know. Even when he talked his way into a classic slow-dance song and spun her on the dance floor, settling into an embrace that made her heart flutter, she was guarded.

He didn't want it to last. So she should appreciate the moment, but that was it.

23

———

Noah
"This narrative wouldn't be terrible," said Grace, "but I'm not sure we're going to be able to spin it correctly when it comes out that the museum is fighting us. Well, you."

Noah's cheeks were still flaming. He'd spent the morning explaining to his parents and siblings that he and Aya were absolutely not a couple, and it had seemed like even baby Hana viewed him with suspicion.

"You're not actually together, are you? High school sweethearts reunited, et cetera. We could you use that."

Noah put his head in his hands. "We weren't high school sweethearts," he said. "I don't know who told you that."

She shook her head. "Only the whole town. Apparently, people were putting bets on you back in the high school years, and some of them are still hoping to cash in. Some people even thought you'd have babies together by now."

He barked a laugh. "Aya definitely doesn't want someone like me. I'm sorry. I assume you know she's working on a doctorate?"

"So she's smart. You're used to smart women."

"Yeah, but she's used to smart men. She'd never want to actually date a college dropout. Nobu warned me about that a long time ago."

Grace didn't bother trying to hide her laugh. "And Nobu was supposed to be some sort of expert, was he?"

"Well, yes. I mean, aren't they all?"

"All gay men? Yep, pretty much. There is not a single gay man on God's green earth whose advice on my personal life hasn't been spot-on."

"Exactly."

"I was being sarcastic, Noah," said Grace, the sweetness of her singsong voice in sharp contrast with the sarcasm that lay buried underneath. Noah was always shocked at how many of his friends thought Grace was a pushover, too kind to do the hard work required of her mishmash of roles. Whereas, in fact, Grace only grew frustrated when people underestimated her. Generally, as long as she was respected, she could appear to be kind and yielding. She didn't mind nearly agreeing with everything, but she always did what she wished.

Noah was a cheap drunk. It had taken him only a couple of years in show business to realize that anything but near-teetotaler status dulled the ambition that was essential to his success. If he relaxed too much each evening and slept in, he couldn't keep up.

But he still loved an occasional glass of whiskey. And Grace, though she rarely had time to drink, was no stranger to hard liquor. So he went to the cabinet where they kept a bottle of the good stuff, poured each of them a fraction of a shot, and raised his glass to Grace.

For the first time that morning, she gave a genuine smile. She closed her laptop, put her phone down, and joined

Noah at the folding table next to the mini fridge. She raised her glass before taking a sip.

"*Kanpai,*" she said. Her Japanese accent was better than Noah's, though she didn't actually speak the language.

"So," he said. "Explain it to me like I'm a total idiot."

She smiled, but he held up one finger.

"Don't," he said, and she nodded.

But her thoughts radiated in her smile. *You are a total idiot, though.* At least she didn't say it out loud.

"Fine. So. Your brother, Nobu, is gay. Did you know this in high school?"

Noah rubbed the back of his head. "Um, no, not really. There were some signs, but I guess I didn't read them very well."

"Good," said Grace. "Signs. Such as what?"

Noah sighed. One shot of whiskey shouldn't have been enough to make him spill all kinds of secrets, but he would have to give Grace something. There had really been one incontrovertible sign, but he had come up with his own explanation.

"Gay porn downloaded onto our computer. I thought it was mine, though."

Grace's eyebrows could have hit the ceiling. "I'm sorry. What?"

"I thought it was mine. So I thought I was gay. You know, like, subconsciously."

She laughed. "I assume you figured things out?"

"Yes. Eventually. I mean, it was a weird time."

"Okay, sure. So you didn't know Nobu was gay, but this porn was on the computer. And you thought maybe it was yours?"

"Like I'd downloaded it in my sleep," said Noah quickly. "Anyway, the point is that Nobu wasn't out to us in high school. So I didn't know, not at the time. But he did give me advice about some things."

"Right," said Grace. "He came out shortly after, right? Sometime in college?"

"Yes," said Noah, remembering that day. It had been strange to see his mother so emotional, terrified for the country and the world that her son was going to be facing. But Grace blazed past it.

"I heard it all from your parents and from Nobu himself," she said, which didn't surprise Noah.

"Nobu had a bunch of weird phases," Grace continued. "He was angry at everyone. Then he was just sad. He never had a romantic relationship that lasted more than a few weeks, but he managed to still have awfully dramatic breakups, and he switched jobs just as frequently."

"That's a little harsh," said Noah. "I switched jobs a lot during those years too."

Grace gave him a pitying look. "Yes, but you were working toward something. If I've read between the lines correctly, Nobu wasn't."

Noah held out his hands. "Look, sure. That's fair."

"So what changed?"

Noah smiled. "Weirdly, it was getting the job he has now. Turns out Nobu just needs to be a dictator."

Grace grinned. "Well, a middle school principal has to be a dictator. So he ended up being a miniature version of your dad?"

"Yep. Turns out they were similar all along. My mom was the only one who really figured that out, though."

Grace clapped her hands. "Excellent. So remember, when we're talking about the Nobu who gave you that advice, the advice about Aya not wanting to date you?"

"Yes. That guy was my brother."

"Your brother. He wasn't exactly a reliable narrator. So maybe that wasn't advice you could take to the bank."

"Meaning?"

Grace shrugged. "Meaning maybe you and Aya actually liked each other then. Maybe things would have worked out if you'd dated. Maybe Nobu was wrong."

"Well, it doesn't matter now. If anything, we're even more different. She's all but finished her doctorate, and I worked a bunch of random jobs instead of finishing college."

Grace nodded. "She is, however, single."

He paused. Grace was never someone to interfere in his love life, not actively, anyway. But sometimes, after he mentioned going on a date that really hadn't worked out, she dropped a comment that had her own opinion hidden in there. He usually chose not to hear.

"You're not serious, right? She doesn't even want to talk to me."

Grace grinned. "Well, you're going to have to talk to someone. Because I just got a call from the president of the museum's board, and they're threatening to blow up our festival."

When Noah started, Grace clarified. "Not literally. But my guess is that, figuratively speaking, the person I spoke to could do some real damage."

"Who is it?" asked Noah, his voice full of trepidation.

Grace grinned. "Oh, it sounds like you already know the answer."

24

Noah

Noah remembered that moment with his brother in the school gym. He had just been slow dancing with Aya, and it was heavenly. The only awkwardness was the pressing need to disguise his tented pants, definitely one of the pitfalls of attending prom with a beautiful girl he had fantasized about for months. After they played "Black is the Color of My True Love's Hair" for the alternative school talent show, he had almost gotten the courage to kiss her. But when he was about to ask her if he could, he was so worried about stuttering that he said nothing. Then one of her friends came by to congratulate them on the performance, and the moment flitted away.

But prom night was famous the world over for being a time when it was easier to confess, kiss, and generally make a fool of yourself. It would be the perfect moment. So Noah bided his time, knowing all he had to do with Aya was write her a note asking her to prom. She wouldn't humiliate him if she said no—she was too kind for that. Thank goodness prom-posals weren't a thing where they grew up.

The prom went almost as well as he had hoped. Aya was gorgeous, and after they took the obligatory photos by the mantelpiece in her mom's house, they were able to drive to the dance laughing and joking like always. She had nixed the idea of eating dinner together, so they had eaten before he picked her up. He jokingly offered his arm, and when she took it, he felt amazing.

But after they arrived at the gym, something changed with Aya. She was more reserved, only reluctantly joining him in ribbing the DJ, who was one of Nobu's old friends and current college classmates, Josh. He wasn't particularly pleased about all the suggestions coming his way.

"It's not my fault your friends want to actually dance, Noah," he'd snapped. "Maybe they don't want a geriatric playlist."

"One slow song," said Noah. "Just make it country. It'll be a crowd-pleaser."

He was pleasantly surprised that Josh chose a good one. Perhaps behind his resentful facade, he was still ready to be kind to his friend's kid brother. But after the song was over, Aya sighed.

"I'm going to go say hi to Emi and Sheena," she said. "Make sure Sheena doesn't overdo it on the vodka, you know."

Noah laughed, though of course he didn't know. "I'm going to go make fun of Nobu's stupid shirt again," he said buoyantly, striding over to the now-abandoned drinks table, where Nobu was sipping a star-spangled cup of his own.

When he got closer, he got a whiff of vodka, making him squint. But that couldn't have been what Aya was talking about, surely.

"Is that, um, a real drink?" he asked.

Nobu nodded. "Confiscated this from some of your

friends," he said. "Don't worry. I won't tell anyone. But in return, don't rat me out."

Noah frowned. "It's probably not a good idea. It's illegal for you, too, you know."

"Let me worry about that. Go enjoy your prom. Show Aya some of those famous dance moves."

Noah must have looked nervous, because his brother laughed. "Don't make such a big deal of it, man. She's a good date for you. Just make sure you don't go thinking it's going to be, like, a lasting thing, just because you like each other now."

Noah bit his lip. "W-Why wouldn't it be?"

Nobu laughed again. "Uh, maybe that she's a genius? She's off to the most prestigious university on the list of places that gave her full-ride scholarships. And come fall, she'll have a boyfriend there. That's how it works. Trust me."

Noah threw a doubtful look at Aya. She was giggling, spinning around with her best friends. Sheena did look rather exuberant, but that didn't necessarily mean she'd had too much vodka. She was always like that. And Emi, who was usually just as studious as Aya, was jumping in the air, laughing.

The way Aya felt about her friends had always been clear to Noah. She loved them all, spent loads of time with them, and would probably always be best friends with them.

But maybe she was about to leave Love Hollow and forget about Noah. He easily saw how that might happen. She'd find a new boyfriend, someone who fit the American ideal of attractiveness—white, tall but not skinny, probably with blue eyes or very light "hazel" eyes. He wouldn't stutter, he would probably have won public speaking contests, and naturally, he'd be great at football. Aya was the whole package: brains, beauty, compassion. *Why wouldn't she end up with someone like that?*

"Thanks," he said to Nobu, though he wasn't feeling very thankful.

Aya wandered back to the drinks table. "Do you want to dance again?" she asked. But she didn't sound as if she meant it.

"No, thanks," said Noah. "I'm not much of a dancer."

25

Noah

Noah went back home to beg for his parents' assistance. It wasn't a great position to be in, but they were the only ones who could help him.

His dad had gone off to work, but his mom was home. She was with little Hana again, scolding the baby for making a mess in her high chair. She had a twinkle in her eye as she chatted, though, which was the way you could always tell her scolding was meant as praise.

But there was no twinkle in Noah's eye. He was furious. "Why did you let Mrs. Irving take over? You might as well put a loaded cannon in charge."

"I'm sorry, son." The "son" was usually a pretty good indicator that she was not sincere. She didn't tend to use that word affectionately, which might have told the casual observer something about her feelings for both her children.

"Well, I'm sorrier. I have no idea why she's making trouble about it now. Again, the festival has been in the works forever."

"Yes, but you only just moved it from the state fair-grounds," said Mrs. Kato. Her eyes, which had been warm as she cleaned her granddaughter's sticky fingers, cooled as she regarded Noah. "So neither Aya nor Mrs. Irving had a great deal of time to adjust to this new reality."

Noah sighed. "I don't know what I was supposed to have done, Mom. The festival's sold out, and there was such a bad rockslide at the fairgrounds we never would have been able to get that area cleaned up."

His mother set aside the miso soup and rice she had been giving little Hana, slipping the tray and the baby out of the device in one smooth series of movements. "You didn't have time to find a solution," she said evenly. "You're going to have to find one now. That's not so unreasonable."

"It is when I can't even talk to Aya," he said. "We need to sit down, look at maps, and go over things face-to-face. But apparently, we can't meet anywhere without it becoming some kind of scandal."

For the first time, his mother gave a genuine smile. "You were a teenager once," she said. "I'm sure you'll think of something."

Nothing was more embarrassing than hearing one's parent allude to anything sexual. At least, that was how Noah had always felt. But his mother did have a point. Parking a car in a secluded spot was not safe for a celebrity, and the A-Wing theater tech booth was definitely out, but only one more private location came to mind.

"I guess we can meet at the cabin," he said. "But I'm going to need some help getting there."

His mother nodded. "How about this," she said. "I'll call your sister. She and I can go there with Hana and get it ready. Nobu can help, too, since he's still preparing it for the engagement party. You set up a meeting with Aya later. We'll make sure it's not a mess anymore."

He frowned. "How much of a mess can it be?"

His family's cabin was a homey place, but it was never untidy.

"You'd be surprised what Nobu has managed to accomplish," she said. "Unlike your father, he doesn't seem to feel a need to work constantly during these summer days."

"He took time off, Mom."

She shrugged. "I'm sure he did, but he needn't spend all of it at the cabin."

"What exactly has he been doing to that place?"

She shook her head. "You'll see soon enough."

26

Aya

Twyla was working, so Emi was the one to drive Aya up into the mountains. The view was ridiculously beautiful, with the mountains all around and the valley looking picture-perfect. Aya tried to look away. People were always talking about that view, as if it made up for the sins of the town's past and present. The legend was that the earliest white settlers had named the place Zion Creek because they felt that such beauty could only have come from God. Of course, they weren't actually the first people there, but the tribal name for the area had been conveniently lost to history. Just as "Zion Creek" would be lost, if that history were not preserved.

Aya had gone back to using the name Zion Creek when she first moved back home. It seemed fitting, somehow, to force the now-infamous name back on the place. But Twyla finally talked her out of it. They had gone to dinner at Chang's, and Twyla was upfront about how she was going to pay so that Aya would be forced to listen to her.

Aya, who did not have a lot of spare cash, had agreed.

But that meant that, even with a table full of delicious food, the meal had gotten off to a difficult start.

"Zion Creek is not accurate," snapped Twyla. "You make yourself sound like a fool, not a historian."

Aya simply raised her eyebrows. "You're not exactly a neutral party. You work for a publication that has the aim of pumping up how supposedly wonderful Love Hollow is."

Twyla glared. "I hope you're not implying that I'm bad at my job."

"No, but part of mine is teaching people what actually happened here. If I go with the postwar-amnesia narrative, accepting the schmaltzy name that the stupid town council thought would be good for tourists, I'm a part of that."

Twyla put down her chopsticks. She took a long swig of tea then sighed. "Do you also go around talking about Prussia, then?"

Aya was silent for a moment. "The town's borders didn't change."

Twyla nodded. "Okay. But the name did. Whether you like it or not, it was officially changed. So if you were doing what most historians do, you'd call it Zion Creek when you're talking about the old town and Love Hollow when you're talking about the modern place. You know, the place where you've spent most of your life."

Aya didn't have a good argument. She added some rice to her bowl then put some of it back. She'd been asking Mama Chang to make brown rice for years, but it never happened. The Changs didn't mind having brown rice at a family dinner, or purple rice, but they were firmly against offering it to customers. Aya, whose culinary education owed more to fad diets than she would like to admit, always felt guilty eating white rice.

"Aya." Twyla added some pea shoots to her plate. "You're not doing yourself any favors here."

"I don't care what people think."

"Well, you should. Because as soon as you call this place Zion Creek, people stop listening to what you have to say. And that's a damn shame."

They ate together in silence for a while. By the end of the meal, they had reached a compromise. Aya would use Love Hollow when talking about the modern town. But if she was giving a talk at the museum, she'd use both. And she wasn't going to keep herself from using phrases like "the town, which has since been renamed Love Hollow" and "the place formerly known as Zion Creek."

As Emi drove, Aya thought about how innocent the town looked. Once you got away from it, the infighting and the small-mindedness, it was finally possible to breathe.

For Aya anyway. Emi looked like she was struggling.

"Are you feeling okay?" asked Aya. Her nerves were jangling from the curves in the road. She had forgotten just how treacherous the route was. When she was a teenager without a healthy sense of fear—in the form of a fully firing amygdala—driving that way in the night seemed vaguely reasonable. As an adult, she was acutely conscious of why the Katos refused to host anyone at the cabin if even a minor spell of bad weather was in the forecast.

Of course, she hadn't checked the forecast. She had been too busy trying to talk Mrs. Irving down. She and the old lady had almost come to blows, and the most she had won was a temporary reprieve.

"I'm fine," said Emi. "A little tired, but that comes and goes."

"No nausea?"

"Not yet," she said. "It'll probably hit me later."

Aya had never had any pregnant friends. The closest she had come were a few coworkers who'd had kids, but she had never been particularly interested in what was going on with them.

"Are you ready?"

Emi smiled. "I should be asking you that. You have to meet a cranky celebrity and solve a huge problem today. I don't have to deliver this baby for almost a year, God willing and Zion Creek don't rise."

It had been their old joke back in high school, and Aya found herself smiling. "Noah's not that cranky. He's just offended that I think his festival is stupid. Why couldn't he have done it back in California?"

Emi shook her head. "Probably too expensive back there."

"Then you charge more," grumbled Aya. "Of course, how would I know? All I've done is run one very small nonprofit into the ground."

Emi was quiet for a moment. "You didn't run it into the ground, Aya."

"But you agree that it's in the ground."

The turns had become hairpins, and Emi slowed as she navigated a tricky one. "Okay. But it's not your job to resurrect the museum, you know."

"How can I ever leave this place if I don't?"

They were close to the cabin. Though they'd passed a couple of homes on the way up, there were no near neighbors. Some of the land was relatively flat, and the Katos had gotten it from the old farmer they used to work for, but everything around it was too steep and rocky for even a tiny dwelling. Though the drive didn't take terribly long, it always seemed to end in the middle of nowhere.

As they got out of the car, Aya admitted softly, "I forgot how beautiful it was."

Spread before them was the whole valley. They could see everything, and the light from the creek glittered in the afternoon sun.

Emi hugged Aya. "Really something, isn't it? It makes me consider moving back someday."

Aya pulled away. "You can't be serious. Has Dr. Flores been trying to recruit you or something?"

Emi grinned. "Yes."

"And are you coming back?"

Emi turned away from the view. "I don't know. What does California have for me really?"

Aya frowned, curious that her optimistic friend was sounded glum. "Music festivals?"

"Not even those."

"Your husband?"

"Yes," she said. Her voice held emotion that Aya wasn't quite sure how to place. She would have expected Emi to be missing Charles, especially since they hadn't seen each other face-to-face since the news of the pregnancy.

"Emi? What's going on with you?"

Noah chose that moment to appear.

27

Noah

Noah saw Aya force a smile as he left the cabin, and Emi's expression looked similarly artificial. He'd always gotten along fine with Emi until prom night of senior year, and even since then, she had never been actively rude. But she looked as if she wanted to cry just at the sight of him.

After much dithering, Noah's dad had finally been the one to give him a ride, and he had arrived at the cabin just as his family was leaving. He'd only just finished going through the fridge when Aya and Emi arrived. Nobu, for all his time in the closet, had apparently turned into a stereotypical fussy gay man at some point during the last decade. The fridge was packed with the finest Japanese and American snacks. They'd even left some hybrids around, like a buttery baked furikake snack his mom had learned how to make from a Japanese Hawaiian friend. Apparently, if Nobu was spending time there, he needed all of those fine things to make himself comfortable.

When Noah invited Aya and Emi to come in, they saw

the results of Nobu's handiwork, and they were just as surprised as Noah but for different reasons.

"How is this whole room a different color?" Emi asked. "I thought your parents would want to keep that old-school wood paneling forever."

"Cheap wood paneling," said Noah. "It really wasn't Nobu's style."

"Isn't your dad kind of sentimental, though?" asked Aya. "He's really okay with all these changes just because Nobu's having a party?"

Noah shrugged. "I g-guess they're glad someone's taking an interest. My sister doesn't like coming up here, and this place is a lot of work."

Emi nodded sagely. "I'm on board with that. Well, I'll let you get to it. These plans aren't going to make themselves. Have fun saving the festival and the museum!"

Aya put a hand on Emi's arm. "Stay for a bit. At least go out on the deck and appreciate the view."

"No, I'd better go. I can't stay too long. Let me know when it's a good time to come get you, Aya."

The drive into town took about forty minutes, and they wouldn't need to meet for more than an hour.

"You're sure you're not going to stay?" Aya asked.

Emi shook her head firmly. "There's some paperwork I need to take care of for my new job. I've been putting it off, but I should really get it done. Besides, your mom said she could come get you."

Aya frowned. "Isn't she teaching tonight?"

"Bye," said Emi firmly, ignoring her question and giving them both a little wave.

Quiet filled the cabin once Emi had left. Noah was with Aya on the side of a mountain—utterly alone.

"So," he said. "I guess we should get started."

Aya, who had gone to the window, nodded. "Yeah. It's just that your mom left these mochi sitting out, so we should probably have some of them first."

His insides uncoiled. If Aya didn't want to deal with the plans, either, at least he wasn't the only person trying to avoid a fight. "Well, if we're eating them, obviously, I have to make tea."

Aya gave a ghost of a smile. "I guess you're the host. So yes, you should be the one to make tea."

She sat there fidgeting while he banged cabinet doors and waited for the water to boil. "Really minimalist," she offered as she looked around the room.

"Yeah, well, it's all Nobu. He said he's going to bring some folding chairs up for the party, but he expects people to be mostly dancing."

"What about the elders?"

"I don't know. He'll just ask them to sit seza? He'd better bring a rug, though. These floors are brutal."

"Yeah," Aya said then took a deep breath. "Want to hear my plan?"

28

————————

Aya

Aya was confused when they left the party. The tradition in Love Hollow was for the teenagers to continue to party the entire night of prom. The compromise that had been reached over the years was that there would be plenty of designated drivers, and any partying would take place at specific homes, not in random places. So Aya and Noah had both been at the nerdier of the large parties. Dane Woodson's parents had opened their house but made it clear that they were staying with a neighbor, and it was where many of the A-Wing kids decamped to after the official dance was over. Many stargazed in the backyard, but because they were the more academically inclined crowd, it involved actual stargazing, complete with an impressive telescope Erica Smith's dad had lent them. The yard was filled with lots of sleeping bags and deck chairs. Many of the attendees had fallen asleep, and as the sun was rising, Noah shook Aya awake.

"Let's go," he said.

She blinked. She had tried to take off her makeup at one

point, but she hadn't done the greatest job with her eye makeup, and her lashes still felt heavy. "Go where? Isn't there going to be breakfast here?"

"I grabbed a couple of things. But I know where we can get a better breakfast."

The car ride up to the cabin was one of the most beautiful of Aya's life. The sunrise, as weak and unimpressive as she had thought it at first, let the light gather in the valley. And for a moment, talking and joking with Noah, she was able to forget Nobu's warning. Of course, he hadn't been the first one to warn her. Noah was an attractive guy, so her senses were already on alert. She had to wonder if he would be like Preston Winters, who had jilted her two years before. Well, not jilted her, not exactly. He'd just flirted shamelessly with her every single day in second period. And since she was an impressionable sophomore and he was a senior, she had made something of it, fully expecting him to ask her to prom. She eventually learned that he had a girlfriend thirty miles away, whom he had conveniently forgotten to mention during every single one of their frequent interactions.

At the time, she'd tried to laugh it off. Her three best friends as well as the twins they sometimes hung around with refused to speak to him. Preston was probably slightly confused though not innocent. He'd most likely convinced himself that he hadn't done anything wrong, and if he'd raised expectations, he seemed ready to forget. But Aya had gotten one clear lesson from that—she was neither pretty nor skinny enough to have a legitimate boyfriend. Guys like Preston would flirt with her, particularly when she was two years ahead in math and could help them with every problem set. But any commitment from them was reserved for the girls who were beautiful and popular. She hadn't been able to see Preston's girlfriend's MySpace page, as it was set to private, but the profile picture was of a blond woman smiling amid a crowd of friends.

The car made its way off the mountain slowly. Noah wasn't a bad driver, although he tended to play his music too loudly. Aya wanted to ask him if he was going to come to her graduation party. But she didn't dare pressure him quite so directly. She would sound desperate.

"Did you change your mind about having a graduation party?" she asked. "My mom was really hoping you'd do it."

He drummed his fingers on the steering wheel, not answering. For a few minutes, on the way out of town, he had held her hand. But now that they were close to the cabin, he kept both hands on the wheel, carefully climbing up from the valley. It was even more exciting than holding hands. Aya had been to the cabin many times, and she knew exactly how abandoned it was.

She was so distracted that she didn't ask Noah again whether he was having a graduation party, though she found his lack of response pretty odd. Nobody loved academics more than the Kato family, and it was unfathomable that they would want to skip that milestone.

When they got there, she went over to the deck as he unlocked the doors. She didn't want to go in at that moment, when the sunlight was at its most beautiful. She was wearing fleece leggings under a formfitting red dress, one that worked with a black cardigan over it. All of her friends had also planned party outfits for post-prom celebrations, as Idaho nights were too cold to wear a prom dress, even with a good jacket. The May sun had started bringing a touch of heat into the day, so Aya unzipped her jacket. Noah walked over then placed his hand on hers.

She looked up at him.

His embrace took her by surprise, his touch decisive but respectful.

"Aya," he began then seemed to be having trouble getting the next word out.

But she didn't have to be a psychic to guess what he had been going to ask.

"Yes," she said, "you can kiss me."

Then she made the decision for him, kissing him with her back pressed against the railing, the rising sun and her own feelings warming her.

They were teenagers, so for what felt like an eternity, they only kissed. There was none of the urgency that a suaver person would have had to break away or change it up or do anything to alter the insane moment in which they found themselves.

But eventually, Noah broke away and led her inside to the couch. Aya had a jittery feeling in her heart. She'd had crushes before, and that hadn't been her first kiss. But it was the first time she had even considered progressing to anything else. She wasn't shocked that Noah had kissed her, but she was surprised that she wanted to throw the idea of virginity down into the valley. What was the good of it, when she wanted Noah so badly? She was pulling his body closer, ready to take a step that she both anticipated and feared.

Her jacket was long gone, and moaned. He was just as hot as she was, and just as she was wondering how any of her clothes would come off, he lifted her up.

They sat on the couch like that, facing each other, panting.

"Are you really going to Chicago?" he asked.

It wasn't the question Aya had been expecting. She thought he might have asked something about condoms, and she very much hoped he was better prepared than she was.

"What do you mean?" It took her a moment to tear her mind from the body of the man in front of her. He had not changed into comfortable clothes. Noah always liked to look good, and his tux was still managing that for him. But his tie had come off, and a couple of his shirt buttons had come loose where her hand had been.

"Chicago," she murmured. Then she remembered—the college applications she'd agonized over, all the different ones, and the letters she'd spent weeks writing as she begged for acceptance. She had been interested in going to a prestigious school, as she thought that was where she'd find the most like-minded people, but it had to be one with a good scholarship. Or rather, a great scholarship. Her mom couldn't help much, and she was too scared of debt to rely on loans. She'd finally gotten the scholarship she had dreamed of, and she'd be headed to PHU in Chicago. It had been really exciting when she got that offer, and she'd been thrilled about it for weeks.

But then something more exciting had happened. Though judging from the expression on Noah's face, Aya thought that more exciting thing was over.

"Okay," he said. "I just thought that maybe, you know, you'd stick around for a while."

Aya stared at him. "I mean, you're not."

"W-What?"

"Sticking around. I thought you were going to Idaho State."

He gave a short laugh. He was holding her hands, and she wished he would stop talking. She could accept it if Noah wasn't quite ready to go all the way, but she definitely wanted the kissing to continue.

"I mean, it's a lot closer," he said. "I just think that since you're about to leave, maybe this isn't a good idea."

Aya could tell that, if nothing else, he had been passionately interested in where their encounter was heading. He'd brought her to an empty cabin at sunrise, for God's sake. But now he was looking away, biting his lip.

"Sure," she said. She wasn't going to beg Noah for anything. If he wasn't even interested enough to hook up with her, she couldn't expect him to make some big declarations about his feelings. She had thought he really liked her, maybe even loved her, their childhood understanding growing into a foundation for something deeper.

But she'd been wrong about guys before—and not just Preston. So she zipped her down jacket up, ignored the lump in her throat, and tried to feel relieved. "Should we go back down to the valley now? I want to get some actual sleep."

29

———————

Aya

"Okay, here's what I envision. The festival is inevitably going to disrupt the Pilgrimage. I mean, the stages are truly in our backyard. So I would say the following— just make sure that, during the religious ceremony, there's not loud music playing. In fact, if you can get people to vacate the grounds during that time, that would be ideal."

"You'll have to do that during the morning, then," said Noah. "Music starts at ten for the early birds, so if it's completely done by nine, it's not going to be that loud. Although we will need to be doing sound checks at both stages."

She shook her head. "That's absolutely not going to work," she said. "We've had the schedule out for ages. The Shinto guy is only going to be here for a couple of hours on Friday afternoon. He has a wedding planned in the morning and an evening plane ticket."

Noah crossed his arms. "Okay. Then there's going to be music during the ceremony. You'll just have to do it inside."

The thought of the moving cemetery being forced into a messy room complete with folding chairs made Aya incensed. The sight of deep-blue sky, the mountains, the haunting beauty the internees would have seen—it was all central to the ceremony.

"I don't understand why this didn't occur to you," she said. "That's what makes me angry. Why did I have to come to you with this? How did you decide to move the festival, not even once considering the museum?"

"I didn't know what week it was," he snapped. "I don't even live here anymore."

"Yes, that's part of the problem."

"I had to l-leave!" he shot back.

She was surprised he was stuttering. Usually, when Noah was angry, he stopped stuttering. It was one of the things that she hated about his moods. She loved listening to the real Noah, the guy who joked and stuttered. She hated the angry, ranting guy with fluent speech. But apparently, that was who she was going to be speaking with, as he was still going on about it all.

"I left because I couldn't stand to be here anymore," he said. "And you know what? Given what's happened to my parents and to the museum, I think I was right."

Aya clenched her fists. She knew very well what the concentrated campaign to close the museum and demonize the Katos had done. In fact, as the person picking up the pieces at the museum itself, she understood the fallout better than anyone else. But it was senseless to pretend that by running away from Idaho at the first possible chance, she'd had no part in that.

"Noah, those things happened in part because you left. And because I left. And Emi and Celine—I mean Chen and Sheena and all of the dumpling crowd."

She was so flustered that she'd used the name Chen had gone by before she moved to California and started to embrace her Chinese roots. Aya was irritated with Noah, but she liked that she didn't have to explain her high school group to him. He'd always understood why the only four Asian girls in their grade had banded together and why the only four Asian girls two grades down had liked to tag along. If anything, he was jealous, as only Nobu had understood what he was going through in high school.

"Why do you think Twyla moved back?" she asked, trying again. "And Nami and me. Who are we if we just abandon this town?"

Noah looked away. "A lot of people did that after Zion Creek," he said. "And you know what? I think their grandkids are probably doing better than we are."

Aya sighed and looked out at the valley. Though the summer days were long, she guessed there would only be about two hours of daylight left, and she and Noah still hadn't reached any kind of agreement. Maybe that wasn't going to happen. She could just go back down, admit defeat, and let Mrs. Irving fight the battles for her.

It sounded kind of nice.

"I'm calling my mom," she said. "If you're not going to give any ground, I may as well leave."

"Fine," he muttered and took out his phone.

They heard the first drop of rain at the same time. Soon, it was all they heard. Their eyes met, and Aya was speechless for a moment.

If the rain continued, they wouldn't be able to leave.

30

———

Noah

Aya was outside, having a conversation, pacing slowly and shaking her head.

Noah's conversation with his parents was, he suspected, very similar to hers.

"Mom, why didn't you tell me it was going to rain? For that matter, why didn't Nobu?"

"I thought Grace would have told you," she said. "As a matter of fact, if she had, you could have been back by now. Are you sure she didn't mention it?"

Noah thought back to the morning's conversations with Grace. The festival had been all they talked about, really. She'd insisted that they press on without worrying too much about the stories in the news, so Noah was trying to do that. In fact, a part of him was relieved. Every time he saw something about himself and a beautiful woman, he became a little less worried. Maybe the media would never discover his secret, especially if he never told another living soul. And even if they did figure it out, they wouldn't have proof. Of course, they were fairly good at going forward without proof of anything. He had learned that the hard way when the publicity around his second album suffered. Apparently, according to the news outlets, Noah was a real diva on tour. But that wasn't his perception at all. As it turned out, all you had to do was find multiple people willing to corroborate such a story, pay them well, and keep a hefty fund to defend against libel lawsuits.

"Well, Grace didn't check it," he said, though it was highly uncharacteristic of Grace to leave him unprepared. "When are you going to be able to come up and get me out?"

He heard his dad in the background probably playing with Hana. His parents had practically adopted that baby by now. Noah wondered again why his sister had bothered having kids if she just wanted to head off and do other things all summer.

"It doesn't look great tomorrow," said his mother. "In a couple of days, certainly."

"A couple of days?"

"Don't blame me," she said sharply. "We went to a lot of trouble getting that place ready for you. It's not as if you're going to starve."

"Yes, there's food, which I guess is good since I'm stranded. Don't you think that maybe Nobu could—?"

But his mother had already ended the call.

"So much for filial piety," he grumbled. "Not sure if you're supposed to keep it up when there's a sheep thief around."

Aya was coming back in, a dark expression on her face, but she gave him a quizzical look. "Sheep thief?"

"Oh, just the old Confucian question. What is the best way to show filial piety if your parent is doing something terrible like stealing sheep?"

"Well, what's the answer?" Aya asked, sitting down at one of the bar stools by the kitchen counter.

Noah shrugged. "My dad could tell you. I was never really interested in that lecture. And now we're stuck here. I expected my parents to at least look at the weather. They never come out here without knowing the forecast at least a week in advance."

"Maybe this is their way of passing the baton to the younger generation," said Aya, and Noah grinned.

"How many batons has your mom passed to you?"

Aya seemed to think about it for a moment. She had told Noah that her mother cooked constantly, took care of everything around the house, and ran a small business single-handedly, doing all of the admin and instruction for her dance studio. The only thing she was willing to outsource was gardening, as she liked having fresh vegetables around but had always relied on her parents for their help with weeding until they got too old. "Yeah, good point."

31

———————

$\mathbf{N}$oah
Noah went outside again, that time to take a call from Grace. It was a shame, since he had just been getting close to a conversation with Aya. He wondered if the foibles of their aging parents might have been enough for him to get through to her. *That stupid little ceremony!* He had thought it was sweet when he was younger but had never thought it would disrupt his life quite so much.

"Winter called," Grace said.

Noah's accountant was clever and soft-spoken, seemingly much more conventional than the crunchy parents who had decided to name their three daughters after different seasons. At least they never had a fourth, so there was no Spring. Just Summer, Autumn, and Winter, the youngest.

"Ok-k-kay," he said. He seemed to be entering another phase of stuttering more. What most of the people around him didn't understand was that his likelihood of stuttering rose and fell, changing day by day and week by week, often not at all tied to whether he was nervous.

But he *was* nervous. Calls from Winter were never a good thing. She lived by her spreadsheets, so it wasn't great news if she had picked up the phone.

"She's not thrilled, Noah," said Grace. "Why didn't you tell me that the festival was supposed to make up such a big part of your living expenses?"

Noah ran a hand through his hair. He would have loved to say he was staying with his parents to help them out. In fact, that was what he had been saying, especially when his California friends teased him for snoozing in what used to be the bedroom he shared with Nobu.

But the truth was that he couldn't have afforded lodging, even if the festival and the Pilgrimage hadn't driven up demand. His credit card bills were mounting, and a good deal of what he expected to make from his albums had already gone into the festival. It would have been okay if they hadn't had to move the location at the last minute, but as things stood, he was going to be very strapped for cash in the near future. And if they had a lot of cancellations, he would be shouldering a serious debt.

"It's fine," Noah said. He never thought he would have ended up in that situation. Before he'd become a well-known artist, he thought his album sales would be more than enough to ensure a comfortable lifestyle. It turned out that unless you were the most famous musician in the country, that was never going to be enough. After he gave everyone involved their cut, he had enough to live modestly in LA, and he was always looking for ads and sponsorships to make up the difference. But they often didn't like his requirements, which included never speaking more than one word. Just the thought of recording an ad with his stutter made Noah both anxious and angry.

"It'll be fine," he said again. "A lot of successful businesses end up being in the red for the first few years."

Silence followed. "Noah, you pay me well," said Grace. "But I hope it's not at the expense of your ability to eat."

"My parents will feed me," Noah said. What was left unspoken was that he really hoped they would keep housing him, too, as not having to pay as many bills for his primary residence was helping him stay afloat. The mortgage on his house in LA was insane, in part because he had felt compelled to go to a neighborhood that was "quiet" for celebrities. That part of the plan had worked, but it also meant he was paying for way more square footage than he needed. And though he had gotten a stylish electric car and a high-end espresso machine, he felt so self-conscious about his income that he found himself hiding half his possessions every time his parents visited.

"Well," Grace said, reading his silence, "how's the negotiation going?"

"Not. Aya won't listen to anything I say. She's gotten so irritated at me for leaving Love Hollow that she's being completely unreasonable, which is crazy, because she left first."

Again, silence came from the other end of the line.

"Well, do what you can," said Grace. "I'll see you tomorrow."

It occurred to him after she ended the call that he hadn't told her he was stranded. Maybe since the darkness was gathering, she had figured that out herself.

32

Aya

When Noah came back in from his phone call, he was reserved. Aya had managed to put together some bibimbap from the ingredients they had as a peace offering. The Katos had never been big on Korean food, but something must have changed over the years. Probably, it was all three of their adult children moving away and discovering the joys of kimchi and gochujang. Aya loved the flavors but still couldn't quite handle the heat. It was so spicy that she kept a ramekin of yogurt next to her bowl.

"Shall I fry you an egg?" she asked.

Noah shook his head. "I'm going to have a shower and go to bed. Good night."

Aya heard the shower starting up. That probably wasn't a bad idea. She hoped he didn't use all the water. The bathroom had some complicated setup that involved recycling rainwater for the toilet and some other system for the shower. Aya couldn't remember how it worked, but she did remember the cabin had previously had only cold water.

After Noah made it big in the music industry, he had paid to have something that would heat the water installed, and the Kato family owed their warm showers to him.

Aya mixed the yolk of her egg in with her rice. Her bibimbap really was a masterpiece. Good thing she hadn't added any sauce to the portion she had set aside for Noah. She could eat it herself tomorrow for breakfast before she got the heck off the crazy mountain.

Noah seemed to be taking a long, hot shower. Aya reflected for a bit on what it would be like to easily afford home renovations. Her mother owned her home, but each repair had to be carefully planned. Last time she needed a new roof, the entire process was stressful, and Aya was angry at herself for not helping. Now that they were in their late twenties, her friends were really starting to earn money. Emi was a doctor, Noah was a celebrity, and even Twyla was putting her low salary to work through careful investing. Sheena, of course, was far ahead of all of them, tracking her savings in a carefully balanced spreadsheet so she could retire from a stressful tech job. But Aya was stuck with a salary so low it was laughable and essentially no graduate funding. She thought again about whether she should abandon Love Hollow, but no one would want a washed-up "scholar" who'd whiffed on a PhD in history. Even the people who earned their doctorates often had trouble finding jobs.

At least she was a good cook. She let out a sigh as she finished the bibimbap. It hadn't been too hard to make, as she had been able to put together several side dishes and cooked vegetables. Aya picked up her feet and rested them on the bottom rung of the stool. Nobu's redecorating scheme was interesting, but he should have left some rugs around. The floor of the cabin was freezing, and Aya might have to get over her antislipper sentiments and grab some from the rack the Katos kept just inside the door.

She rooted through the desserts and tried to ignore the sound of Noah's shower ending. For a while, Aya had felt so self-conscious about sweets that she had never eaten them in public. More recently, she had been trying to strike a balance. She had small treats if she happened to go out, but otherwise, she tried to avoid having dessert. She told herself that fruit made up for it and eating something sweeter than a pomegranate was unseemly.

But since Noah apparently wasn't going to speak with her, she would have free rein in the kitchen. Though she couldn't get much of the work done that required her to go online, maybe she could get her notebook out and start working on her remarks for the remembrance ceremony. That was usually one of her favorite parts of the whole Pilgrimage, the chance to sit around a fire and hold the attention of people who understood her past. But that year, she'd been so caught up with the planning that she hadn't gotten a chance to even think about what she was going to say.

She selected a *chawan*, a small plate, that had a cherry blossom design. Onto it she placed one mochi—classic, with red beans as the filling—one gourmet chocolate caramel, and one small piece of matcha-flavored cake roll. *There. Variety, indulgence, but not a huge amount of it.*

Then she sat down again and began massaging her temples. It was going to be a little hard to enjoy the dessert with the storm cloud hanging over the entire cabin. She hadn't expected Noah to stonewall her, had thought that she could lean on their old friendship to make him see reason. But everyone always said that fame changed a person, and it wasn't as if Noah Kato was an exception. It had been a while since he released a new album, and Aya had seen the rumors about that. Apparently, he was too busy dating a variety of gorgeous LA women to work hard on his music anymore. The photos that were taken at a distance were less painful, but Aya hated seeing the ones from social media. So many ladies liked to take selfies of themselves in clothing so sexy it made Aya question all of her life choices. Maybe, if she could only look more like that, she would have a partner—not necessarily a Noah Kato but somebody. Coming back to Love Hollow was strange because she saw lots of her peers who had paired off, even people like her who hadn't dated at all in high school.

Noah appeared in front of her, and she almost jumped out of her chair.

"We have a problem," he said.

Aya eyed him steadily. "Yeah, I know. And we were supposed to have found a solution by now."

"It's not that."

"Great," she said. "Another problem."

"Yeah." He shifted from one foot to the other. Aya was trying not to pay attention to what he was wearing. He'd put on a light-green sleeping yukata with matching pants, and his gorgeous hair was soaked from the shower. Noah never had much facial hair, but he was clean-shaven, which suited him.

Aya got to her feet. "You may as well show me."

33

Noah

Noah gestured toward the full-size bed in what used to be his parents' bedroom. "I guess Nobu left this for himself. Everything else has been cleared out."

"There's the bunk beds in the kid room," said Aya. "I'll just take one of those."

Noah shook his head. "The other bedroom is empty. I don't know why it would need to be. Mom said something about wanting a play space specifically for Hana, but what baby wants to play in an empty room?"

Aya bit her lip. She was already starting to shiver, but she tried to hide it. "Is there a rug in there, at least?" she asked, pretending to be braver than she felt.

Noah sighed. "N-No, he really cleared this place out. There's not even a sleeping bag, and it's freezing."

"Don't you have emergency supplies in your car?" Aya asked. The Katos were fanatical about that. They always had first aid kits that were better stocked than anyone else's.

Noah gave her a look.

"Oh yeah," she said. "No car."

He rubbed his eyes. "Do you mind if I lie down just for a bit? You can get me up, and I'll go in the living room after a few."

Aya took a step back. "It's fine," she lied. "I'll just get ready. We can share it."

Noah didn't answer, and she started to walk away.

"It's not a big deal," she said.

"Wait," he called, and Aya turned around.

Noah had gone into the dresser drawers and offered her a matching yukata set. "I think they're all the same s-size," he mumbled. "We just keep them around so we don't have to bring pajamas up here."

"Thanks," she said delicately.

Aya went back out to the kitchen, biting her lip. If she was going to work it out with Noah, she would definitely need some dessert first.

With her dessert finished, she had her own shower, though she kept her hair dry so she wouldn't be cold all night. She'd never properly slept with Noah, and now she had to worry about whether he would steal the covers. It didn't quite seem reasonable.

When she got to the bedroom, the light was out, and Noah's breathing was even. She picked up the edge of the bedding as if it would scald her. At least the bed seemed fairly well equipped, with flannel sheets and a heavy down comforter on top. She was still a little warm from the shower, though she could feel the air around her getting colder. It might be summer, but the nights could be extremely chilly at that elevation.

The rain slowed on top of the roof until it was just a

gentle patter. Aya listened carefully to its rhythm. If the rain would stop, she could leave in the morning, just as soon as she could convince someone to come get her. Until then, all she had to do was sleep.

34

____

Aya was jolted awake by lightning outside the window. It threw everything into a strange half-light, and she gave out a low moan. Without knowing what had happened, she had grabbed Noah. She could feel the cotton of his yukata, and she forced herself to release her grip. But she couldn't slow her breathing.

"Are you okay?" he asked.

"Yes," she said, but it didn't come out right. "I just don't really like lightning."

"I think that's it for a while," said Noah, but he was wrong.

Aya tried to speak to distract herself. "It's just that it reminds me a little bit of that hike senior year," she managed. "Just, you know, there was lot of lightning that day too."

"That was insane. You all could have been killed."

She didn't tell him she hadn't wanted to go on the hike and had only signed up because she was so confused after prom night that she needed somewhere to put her emotions. She couldn't let her parents—or anyone else—

find out what had happened. She'd given a sanitized version to her friends, telling them that she and Noah had decided to just be friends. It was less humiliating that way. They didn't believe her, clearly, but at least it saved her from some of the teasing. And fortunately, so many people had hooked up and broken up on prom night that any speculation was lost in the cloud of gossip that hung around the senior class like a haze of poison gas.

"I'm okay," she said, trying to convince herself. "I'm safe."

"If Mr. Mettemeyer had been a teacher, he would have been fired," Noah went on. "I can't believe anyone would give a guy like that permission to lead a group hike. He even has a pilot's license, though I guess that shouldn't surprise anyone."

"Please. It really doesn't help me when you say things like that."

"You don't find my anger soothing?" he asked, only half joking.

"No," she said firmly. "Never, in fact."

He shifted, and she thought they might separate, but his arms were still around her. "I'll keep that in mind."

Something in his tone that made her wonder. "What is it, Noah?"

Another pause followed. "Well, you just seem like you've been angry too," he said.

"Of course I'm angry!" she cried. "I've been angry forever, and this week has been a nightmare, honestly."

"The f-festival?"

"I mean, yes, but not just that. Emi being here as well."

"I thought you were still best friends. And you're close with the other gyoza ladies or whatever."

She giggled in spite of herself. "I think you get that name wrong on purpose. We were the dumpling club."

"Okay, the dumpling club. I thought the four of you stayed more or less united."

"Yes. And everyone is worried about me. But nobody lives here or even wants to come back for a visit, so they nominated Emi since she has a break from work for now. And, you know, money."

"Money is useful sometimes," said Noah in a tone she couldn't quite decipher.

"Okay, sure." She leaned her head back, closing her eyes. "I just wish I had more," she mumbled.

Noah was silent, and she felt like he was her confessor. Except that, back when she had actually gone to confession, she'd always hated it. She used to invent sins to avoid having to share any of her actual life with Father Norton. At the time, she had reasoned that the penance would be similar, so it was justified.

"I'm happy for Emi," she said. "Honestly, I am, but it feels like it's all happened for her. I mean, here we are, ten years out of high school, and she has everything."

Noah sighed. "Not everything."

"Everything," she insisted. "Prestigious degree, dream job, a husband, a house, a car, and now a baby. Check, check, check."

Noah didn't say anything. "It's not too late, though," he said. "Come on, Aya. Especially not for someone like you."

She opened her eyes and looked up at his face. "Sure," she said. "But it could be. I haven't really moved toward any of those things, and now both my job and my degree are potentially down the drain. And you know, a decade of my life. So that night on the mountain could have been life-changing, but it clearly wasn't. Not for me. And now I'm just here, an object of pity for my friends."

"That's probably the wrong word," said Noah.

"You don't pity me?" she asked. Her voice was trembling again.

In the faint moonlight, she could see his wide grin. "You're smart, you're generous, and you're beautiful," he said. "No, Aya. No pity here."

All of a sudden, his face was closer to hers, his arms tight around her, and she had to catch her breath. Noah Kato was dangerous for her. If she let herself get any ideas, she was going to be stuck trying to rid her mind of him for at least another decade.

Still, she kissed him. It was incredible.

She was more attracted to him than ever. Back on prom night, even the kissing had been a little awkward. Neither one of them had been experienced, and Aya had found herself scared and excited in equal parts about the actual logistics of what was supposed to follow.

But she didn't need to give in to worries like that anymore. The night when she'd lost her virginity sophomore year of college to a guy in her study group had not been unpleasant, if slightly underwhelming, and she'd had many experiences since then that helped her figure out what she liked. And she definitely liked the way Noah was kissing her. Aya found herself fumbling with the tie on his yukata, cursing his neat little knots.

She loved what she saw. Noah Kato didn't do shirtless photos. Aya had looked for them, though she never admitted it to anyone. He had shown off his arms in sleeveless shirts for certain magazines, though. She loved his tattoos, and she thought she must be the only person who understood all of them. He didn't go in for many tattoos that had Chinese characters, so there were none that appeared in photos, but she knew he had "Fall down seven times, get up eight" written vertically between his shoulder blades.

She'd heard about that one through the grapevine, and apparently, Nami had teased him that he would need a mirror to even remember what was written back there. But Aya, whose family had also embraced the resilience in that motto, had always hoped she would see it.

But at the moment, she was too busy kissing him to go investigate his back tattoo.

Then a memory hit her, and she stopped. "Maybe this isn't a good idea."

He pulled back, staring into her eyes. "What?"

"That's what you said to me," she said. "Last time we were here."

His arms were still around her, and he moaned. "I was hoping you would contradict me," he said.

She snorted. "Are you serious right now, Noah Kato? You were hoping I would tell you you were wrong?"

"Yes."

"You needed more confirmation or something?"

He stroked her hair. "I mean, I think I was still kind of taken in by the Catholic thing. Do you know what Father Giacamo told us?"

Aya put a hand over her eyes. "Do I want to know? Okay, fine. Tell me."

He stroked her stomach through the yukata, and she tensed up. "That if we had relations with a young woman, we should come beg her for her forgiveness. Because tempting her into sin was sinning against her, and we had no right to inflict that on someone."

She sighed. "I'm so glad your family isn't Catholic anymore."

Pulling her hands back down, gazing into his eyes again. "So you wanted me to overcome your resistance," she said, a smile tugging at the corners of her mouth. "I think I might be able to do that."

She reached down, but he grabbed her wrist. "There's something you should know."

"What?" She felt impatient. The moment had some sort of wedding-night feeling to it, like they had gone through a whole production, and they were finally ready to reap the private reward. Of course, it was a dance that had gone on for years, starting when they were much younger.

"That night," he said, "w-well, for me, it had a r-really big impact."

She loved it when he stuttered. To Aya, Noah's voice when he was stuttering was at its most beautiful. With the world outside, he was the famous Noah Kato, never deigning to say more than a few words. And if he did have to speak in public, he busted out every possible trick he could to avoid stuttering. He never introduced himself or his band members by name, for example. He called them something different every time. He never called himself Noah but said, "I'm your young lover," or "I'm a fool with a guitar," or even, "I'm a man who thinks the ladies in the front row here at Jo-Jo's look *fucking amazing!*"

Aya had watched that video more than once. It always put her in a bad mood.

But when he stuttered with her, he was showing her he was comfortable. He trusted her, and letting her hear his thoughts was the most important part, not hiding his stutter.

"What is it?" she asked, still impatient.

"Um, so, I never really came b-back from that," he said. "I've never had sex."

Aya's first reaction was to laugh. She couldn't stop herself. The more she laughed, the more the merriment seemed to take over her whole body. He had said it with such sincerity too.

"Noah, please. I'm not a virgin, either, obviously. You don't have to say things like that!"

When he didn't respond right away, she kept chuckling, but then her laughter died.

"Wait. You can't be serious."

"W-What? Is it so unbelievable?"

Some of her anger came back. "I mean, yes! You're always in the tabloids with some hot woman. They speculate all the time about how much play you must be getting."

"By design," he said quietly.

"How come nobody has talked?" she asked, still peering at him. She didn't think Noah would actually lie to her, yet it was at odds with the image he'd projected for years, so she couldn't quite believe it.

"And say what? 'Noah and I had a nice time, but he dropped me off at my door'? Even if one person told the tabloids that, they wouldn't believe it. And they certainly wouldn't think it was true for absolutely everyone."

"But there would be a rumor, something like that. Wouldn't they decide you're gay?"

He grinned. "Well, I'm not," he said, leaning in to kiss her neck. "I mean, there are plenty of ladies who know *that* much."

His kisses took her breath away for a minute, then she took one of his hands in hers.

"So, is this really okay, then?" she asked. Maybe there was more about him she hadn't realized. If he was secretly a virgin, he could secretly also be a Buddhist monk or something. "What were you waiting for?"

"You," he said then kissed her again. "I was waiting for you."

35

Noah

The morning dawned, the sun shining in a cloudless sky.

Noah pulled the curtains shut and made the bed bounce as he leaped back into it. Aya let out a sleepy giggle, and he thought it might be the single most alluring sound he had ever heard.

Hours later, even the heavy blue-and-white curtains did nothing to hide the excellent weather. With a moan of regret, Noah raced off to look at his phone, which just had a text from his musician mentee, asking if he could call later in the day. He'd expected someone from his family to check in, at least to make sure they still had power, but there was nothing.

Aya's eyes were closed.

"Are you still asleep?" he ventured.

She smiled. "No, but I could use some coffee."

They had their coffee out on the porch, watching the valley come alive with late-morning activity. A bird feeder had apparently done an excellent job of keeping the birdseed dry, as a parade of finches and sparrows braved their company in order to eat from it. It was almost warm enough for them to sit in their yukata, but Noah had found an old cardigan his grandmother had once made in a bag meant to protect it from moths. It smelled of cedar. Though Noah had made fun of the cable-knit pattern when he saw his father using it, Aya looked absolutely gorgeous—and happy, too, sipping her coffee as she warmed her fingers on the mug. They were in one of the Adirondack chairs, but he'd brought out the outdoor cushions to make it more comfortable.

It occurred to him that he'd located many things that could have helped him make an alternate sleeping arrangement the previous night. The cardigan, the cushions, the cozy wool blanket that was covering both of them as Aya sat in his lap. Good thing he hadn't thought of any of it.

"Is this what your house is like?" asked Aya suddenly. "An incredible view, like this one?"

Noah laughed. "My house has the opposite of a v-view," he said. "Just a huge fence surrounding all the sides."

She looked disappointed. "Oh. I guess I picture all of LA as a giant beach."

"You're a historian. Aren't you s-supposed to know geography?"

Her features clouded. "Of course. But I'm not necessarily an expert on the current LA housing market."

"That's a shame, because I might sell m-m-my house. I could have used an expert."

She leaned against his shoulder, and he kissed the top of her head. He noticed himself stuttering more, probably because he was so sleep-deprived. The feeling of Aya in his arms was electrifying. Perhaps he would never sleep again.

"Don't you like where you live?" she asked, tracing one of the cardigan's embossed buttons with her finger.

He shook his head. "Not really. It's expensive and also boring. The worst of both worlds."

"Must be nice to own your own place, though."

He snorted. "Hardly. I'd say it's really overrated."

She sat up slightly, placing her coffee on the arm of the chair. "Well, I suppose if you can afford to decide, that in itself is a good thing."

He put his own coffee down. "I guess. Theoretically. Breakfast?"

She nodded, getting unsteadily to her feet. "I'll cook if you keep the coffee coming. I don't even know what to make. Your family left so much food here."

"Yeah," said Noah. "It's a crazy amount, right?"

A grin crept across her face. "I suppose. Noah, do you know whether your family checked the weather?"

"They didn't."

"My family didn't either. Emi usually looks at her weather apps pretty constantly. Apps, because she has more than one. That's how much she likes being up on the latest forecast."

He heaved himself out of the chair then took her hand. They were both beset by laughter.

"I guess I should have realized," he said.

"What?"

"What everyone else has realized." He wanted to add, "I'm in love with you." But he didn't want to face disappointment, not yet. The beautiful woman standing next to him, laughing, might think he was crazy if he said something like that.

So instead, he squeezed her hand. "That you're amazing.

That being stuck in this cabin with you would be the best possible outcome of this meeting."

It was the wrong thing to say. She moaned, closing her eyes. "The meeting. I completely forgot."

He was disappointed in himself for getting things wrong, but he pulled her into the cabin. "I'm sorry. Let's wait until we have breakfast ready. Then we can talk."

36

—————

Noah

Noah felt like he was floating when Emi dropped him off at his parents' house. He'd gone up the mountain feeling the weight of his responsibilities, but his lens had shifted, and he couldn't believe his good luck. Even his parents' house, as humble as it was, looked beautiful to him. The garden was immaculate, the garage door freshly painted, and the gravel next to the basement windows neatly raked.

"Hi, Noah," said their neighbor Stacy. She was in her sixties and had worked in one of the two public preschool classrooms for many years. Noah had heard enough about the way she'd been treating his parents to be wary of her. Stacy looked every inch the kind, respectable neighbor, wearing sweatpants and an old Love Hollow Bucks shirt as she worked in her garden. In fact, once upon a time, she used to be rather kind. Every time she talked about her work, she seemed both proud and angry, but apart from that, she was okay. She was strict about only letting the kids have one piece of candy each on Halloween, but at least she didn't run out, and she never failed to say hello.

At the moment, though, Noah didn't want to talk with her. He only raised his eyebrows and nodded, giving a dim imitation of a smile. It usually worked in LA when he wanted to stop talking to someone, but it didn't seem to have the same effect in Love Hollow.

"The weather looks great for the festival," she said. "My nieces are going, and I even got a senior ticket one day."

Then you lied about your age, Noah thought. *Either when you bought the ticket or two years ago, when you claimed to be in your fifties.*

"Good to hear it," he said carefully, giving her the smallest of waves before he let himself into the house. For a moment, his mood crumpled. He had pictured the festival as an event that would bring people together. And unfortunately, there didn't seem to be a way of keeping people like Stacy out. He should talk to Grace about her ticket, though. If it had been a fraudulent purchase, maybe they could send her an email. Dear Valued Customer: *It has come to our attention that there has been an error in the purchase price of your ticket. A discount that was meant to be applied only for senior citizens was added to your ticket.* Lots of passive voice to make her think it had been generated automatically.

"*Tadaima,*" he said, his voice slightly hushed.

"*Okaeri!*" Since only his father replied, he imagined his mom must be off somewhere.

In the living room, which had apparently been converted into a baby room, his dad was on the floor once again. Baby Hana was drooling and smiling.

Noah, still unsettled by his brush with Stacy, frowned at the sight.

"So, are you and Mom the full-time help now? Does Nami ever s-see her kid?"

"She does" came a response from the kitchen.

Noah's mother and sister came into view.

"Sorry, Nomnom," said Noah immediately, but the damage was done. His sister was scowling.

"Are you sad that Hana replaced you as the baby of the family?" she asked sarcastically, scooping up Hana and settling her on her hip. "Wish that Mom and Dad would still think of you as not fully capable of, I don't know, wiping your own nose?"

She daubed at Hana's nose as she said it. Hana squirmed, and her grandmother stepped in immediately.

"I'll take her out back," she said. "You two, have a cup of tea."

Noah scowled at his sister. "No, thanks. I'll watch Hana for a minute."

"Why don't you entertain her with a song instead," said their father. He had always been the peacemaker, which sometimes bothered his wife.

But she nodded approvingly. "Yes. We're storing so many musical instruments for you in our basement. Go get one and make yourself useful."

"I told you that you could sell those," Noah said, rubbing his neck as he went down the stairs.

"They feel weird about it!" Nami yelled after him. "Here, buy this cheap mandolin, once used by the famous Noah Kato. You should sell them yourself."

"I don't want them," Noah grumbled, though he was out of his sister's hearing. The basement was full of things, but they were carefully organized, so he was able to find the corner with his instruments easily. They were neatly arranged next to a tower of book boxes.

He went back upstairs with a guitar. It had been his first instrument, apart from the cellos that had introduced him to music, and he still felt sentimental about it. For years, he could spend hours on the guitar, playing his favorites and noodling away. It was the very instrument he had used for that rendition of "Black is the Color of My True Love's Hair" with Aya in high school, the one that had almost led to his kissing her before he lost his nerve. He sat down on the playroom floor, where his family was assembled, and played the first few chords of that song. It lifted his spirits instantly. But not wanting them to ask about Aya or know what he was thinking, he quickly switched to "Slumber My Darling" and smiled when he saw Hana gurgle. It would be a good lullaby for her.

For the next half hour or so, his whole family was happy. Noah was surprised by how much he had missed playing. The festival included him and his band, of course, but he'd intentionally packed their set with songs they could play in their sleep, so he hadn't been practicing much. And keeping Hana entertained was its own challenge, requiring him to play lots of nursery songs by ear and change his expressions with her. He even started writing a song about a teddy bear she had been mouthing.

"That wasn't bad," said Nami as she was getting ready to take the baby home. "You should write more songs and record them. If it wouldn't be hard for you to do that."

Noah followed with a technical explanation of what recording considerations a person might need when recording songs for a children's album.

Nami burst out laughing. "Do all singers know that stuff, or are you just a nerd?"

Noah shrugged. "Everyone has some idea of the basics. I mean, you have to. You can't risk sounding terrible. But I'm more interested in the details than most artists. Usually, the guys recording me either love me or hate me."

"Guys? Don't tell me they're all guys."

"I mean, there are women who can do the work. But they don't tend to get hired. So yes, mostly guys."

Hana took the baby from their dad, tucking her into some kind of body sling with an agility that Noah thought he would never be able to match. "Shame. I wish we could dismantle the patriarchy before this one comes of age, but it seems unlikely."

"Yeah," said Noah.

Hana was suddenly limp and tired. He felt the same way and touched her fuzzy head.

"Thanks, Han-Han," he said.

Nami looked at him, suspicious. "New nickname?"

"Yes. After her mom."

After a pause, Nami gave a grudging smile. "I like it."

After she left, the house seemed empty again. Noah went off to his room for a nap but found himself waking up quickly. The thoughts of Aya were too strong, too persistent. He needed to be with her again. Immediately.

37

Aya

Aya couldn't help feeling buoyant as Noah left. She scowled a bit as she saw him talking to his neighbor, Stacy. Then again, the Stacys of Love Hollow weren't the main problem. Aya had talked at length with her several times, as they somehow seemed to end up paired together at volunteer events. The annual fundraiser for the local art center was a good example. Aya had always hated attending the event, which was a debutante ball in all but name. The sight of all of the young women in white gowns, getting ready to dance with their fathers was just weird. But she didn't mind taking tickets at the front, and Stacy was with her.

That was before the whole mess with the museum, of course, so they spoke pretty freely about other subjects. Aya was amazed by how much Stacy hated her job. She seemed to like kids, so perhaps she wasn't a terrible teacher, but she went on at length about systemic problems and her specific problems with most of her coworkers. When Aya gently brought up the subject of a career change, Stacy completely dismissed it. She already had her degree, thank you, and had absolutely no plans to make any changes.

It was a little hard to admire someone like that. Then again, Aya had a creeping feeling that she had the same problem. For a long time, she'd lacked the courage to finish her PhD. But that could all end. Aya decided that she would call her advisor again that day. There was no use putting it off. She could take the next couple of years to finish while staying in her role at the museum then look for a teaching job. It would be hard to do it all long-distance, especially when she'd all but stepped away from her research, and it would require her saving the museum.

But that morning, she felt like she could do anything.

"So?" asked Emi.

"So what?" asked Aya.

Emi dutifully put on her blinker, pulling into the parking lot of an abandoned church. Typical Emi. She signaled even when there was nobody around.

"I'm going to ask you again," said Emi. "Only don't play dumb with me this time."

After a long silence, Aya nodded. "Yes."

Emi gasped. "Yes?"

"Whatever question you were going to ask, I think the answer is yes," said Aya, blushing furiously.

Emi laughed. "I knew it! Twyla thought you would be too stubborn, but I knew you'd fall for him. Noah Kato, who you definitely weren't ever thinking about. Ha!"

Aya sighed. "So you and Twy put bets on it, huh?"

Emi shook her head. "I'm about to have a very nice income, thank you very much. I refused to take Twyla's money. It would have been too easy."

She reached into a cooler bag next to her feet and brought out two plastic bottles of green tea. "Here, take one.

I think we should be having champagne, but I can't, for obvious reasons."

Aya accepted it gratefully. "Oh, thank God. I could really use this. I'm so tired."

Emi laughed again. "I'm sure you are."

Aya was still blushing. "Okay, okay. But tell me how you knew."

Emi tilted her head. "I mean, how could I not have known? That's the question. You've been in love with him ever since that talent show. 'Black is the color of my true love's hair?' Come on."

Aya paused. She lowered her green tea bottle. "Back then, it wasn't love," she said carefully. "It was lust. Noah wasn't in love with me."

"And you?"

Aya found she couldn't answer. "It doesn't matter now. Anyway, I don't even know what happened yesterday." She could have added that what had happened had been repeated more than once in the morning, but she and her friends had never been that explicit. Maybe it was because their attitudes had crystallized in high school, when only one of them had dated. It still felt strange. If Emi had decided to have a bachelorette party, it probably would have been the tamest thing ever, as Sheena was the only big drinker and nobody would have had the nerve to buy penis candy.

"So you don't know where you stand?" said Emi. "I mean, that's normal. If it were an actual date, you probably wouldn't even be talking about exclusivity now."

Aya groaned. "I don't think I'm a good fit for dating anyone where that isn't, like, implied."

"But I thought you hooked up with that hot guy from Bremen. The one who was poly, who had that primary partner in New York."

Aya shook her head. "Please don't remind me about Marcus. There are many reasons I didn't become his secondary partner. Or tertiary partner. Or Chicago side piece. I don't know. The whole thing just wasn't for me."

Emi patted her arm. "Well, whatever. You and Noah will figure it out. You were made for each other."

She put the car back in gear and pulled out of the parking lot carefully. Her words had made Aya thoughtful.

"Do you think that exists?" she asked. "You know, soulmates?"

"For the two of you? Definitely."

"No, really," said Aya, watching as they drove past their old middle school. It looked sad, abandoned in the middle of summer. The district had never been able to afford air-conditioning for most of the buildings, so on average days, they were fine, but if they happened to have a warm September, the classrooms were miserably hot. "Do you feel like Charles is the one person for you?"

Emi touched the edge of her right eye with her sleeve. "You make your own soulmate," she said stiffly.

"What? Like, out of clay?"

"It's like making your own luck. If you live with someone for decades, take care of them, share everything with them."

"Have a child with them?" asked Aya, hoping to cheer her friend up.

But Emi only gave a small shrug. "Sure, raise a kid with them, possibly. All of that? It adds up. And that person becomes your soulmate."

"Well, I don't know if Noah's going to be quite up for a conversation about growing old together and having a bunch of grandkids we spoil abominably, et cetera," she said, and Emi smiled again. "Especially because he thinks that his parents are spending too much time with Hana."

That was safer territory, and Emi actually laughed. "I stopped myself from saying it earlier, but I'll say it now. Men don't know anything, do they?"

"No," said Aya, glad to see the familiar sight of her mother's house coming into view. "They really don't."

38

———

Aya

Emi and Aya were alone when they arrived, so Aya decided to seize the moment. She could head to the museum later. After two years of putting in more than full-time hours, she could use a tiny bit of the flexibility that was supposed to be one of the benefits of the job.

She was lucky, and Professor Jin answered on the first ring.

"I'm glad I caught you, Professor," she said, almost breathless. "I've been thinking, and I want to go over a plan to finish my dissertation. I know my progress hasn't been great, but I'm thankful that you didn't give up on me. And I'm not going to throw this opportunity away."

A moment of silence followed. "So you got my email?"

No, I didn't, Professor. I was spending every waking moment with the same celebrity who earned me a mention in all of America's trashiest publications.

"I haven't been getting good internet," she said. "I'm sorry. Could we go over it now?"

Professor Jin sighed. "The blessing and the curse of not

being near campus," she said. "Our new president is cutting the entire department."

Aya just managed not to laugh. It wasn't the kind of thing Professor Jin would joke about.

"Even American History?" she asked weakly.

"Especially American History. Seems he doesn't take too kindly to anything negative being said about the United States. So Japanese American internment, naturally, is not his favorite topic. He would rather all talk of the Second World War be limited to D-Day and, perhaps, Rosie the Riveter."

Aya's heart fluttered. She had been blissfully going through her life, thinking the only place where she would face racist suppression of her research would be in Love Hollow. As it turned out, far away at a well-regarded Eastern university, the same thing was about to happen.

"So what happens to my doctorate?"

"If you come back to campus, you can try to finish it in a year. You won't get any more time than that. Ten months from now, I will be out of a job."

"They have to find something for you!" cried Aya. Professor Jin was a coup, a genius. She had turned down a great deal of attractive offers because she was loyal to their university, thanks to a scholarship she had received as an undergrad. *And now this?*

"I would prefer that you not worry about me, Aya," said Professor Jin, her voice steely. "I have a great deal of research and teaching experience under my belt. But it is very important that you decide on your own course of action."

Aya went back to what she had just heard her mentor say. "I'm sorry. You said if I come back to campus. I can't work remotely?"

"Absolutely not," said Professor Jin. "That's been made very clear. To all of us."

Finding it difficult to breathe, Aya managed to say, "Okay. Thank you."

The harshness of Professor Jin's voice lessened a notch. "Give yourself time to think on it, Aya. I know you have family obligations, and you may not have warm feelings toward the sort of university where this kind of thing happens. Though I fear that may be more and more places as time goes on."

"*Yare-yare*," muttered Aya.

"Quite," said Professor Jin drily. "Though I'm afraid it's likely all the same."

"Okay. Thanks."

When she put down her phone, the world seemed to have shifted. She went to the kitchen, poured the rest of her green tea into a glass with ice, and went to the back window.

This is not going to be an easy choice.

39

———————

Aya

Aya had made so many calls to the museum's plumber of choice, Nathan, that they should have been good friends. But he had a tendency to answer in monosyllables, so that seemed to thwart even her most polite attempts at conversation.

"So, do you think you can fix it?" she asked, trying not to reveal the level of nervousness she was feeling.

"Eventually."

She bit her lip. "How late is eventually? Because we have a bunch of people coming in."

"A month, maybe two."

He had already told her the work would take time and a lot of parts would need to be replaced. But she had been hoping there was some way to fast-track that.

"Okay. Do you know if any of the bathroom rental places could get us something last minute, then?"

That time, he didn't say anything, only shook his head.

"Are you sure?"

"Festival."

Of course. They had probably rented all the facilities within a hundred-mile radius. There she was, basically solely responsible for providing bathrooms to dozens of senior citizens, and she had absolutely nothing.

"Thanks, Nathan."

"Welcome."

He cleared out, and Aya was left standing at the front desk of the museum. Her computer was open, the draft of her thesis outline blinking up at her. It had been hilarious to think she could come in to work late, still exhausted even after all that coffee and tea, and think she could work on it. Not to mention the impossibility of returning to Chicago. Then the museum would be truly abandoned.

Into all that chaos barged Mrs. Irving, though Aya was thankful it was in the form of a phone call. Aya sent it to voice mail. She should have learned over the years. Everyone who worked for Mrs. Irving either quit or bowed down completely to her tyranny. Aya didn't think of herself as working "for" anyone, but it turned out that when Mrs. Irving was on the board, everyone was at her beck and call. Her mother always said they should be thankful, that if someone had to take the place of both Katos on the board, it needed to be someone who was well known in Love Hollow.

She didn't say "well liked," as that would have been a bit of a fib. Mrs. Irving was well known. Perhaps, in the words of some people, she was infamous.

And she was knocking on the front door.

"We're closed today," said Aya, unlocking it and opening it just a crack. It turned out there was a reason that was not recommended. She should have written a message and slipped it under the locked door, the way she was always told to do in little booklets about preserving her civil rights.

Because an unlocked door, to Mrs. Irving, was an open

invitation. In spite of the warm afternoon, she was dressed in sensible pumps, tights, and a gray wool suit with a well-ironed blouse underneath. Small studs were in her ears, her hair in her trademark braided bun. Aya never pictured Mrs. Irving any other way. She wore the same outfit for a shift selling nachos at the football game as she did when she gave a eulogy at a funeral. And she gave plenty of those. Mrs. Irving was always willing to help and always eager to talk, so when there was no other obvious speaker, the role often fell to her.

"I've come about the flowers," she said. "I saw that you forgot to order them for the festival."

Her voice had more than a bit of an English accent left in it, though she'd lived in the United States for most of her life. Aya always suspected her of putting it on a bit. After all, it made her sound even more imperious and somehow smarter than her listeners.

"You have a copy of the budget, Mrs. Irving," she said. "There wasn't any money left for flowers this year."

"Yes, I have a copy of the budget," she said. "Did you ask any of the local florists for donations?"

"Hmm? Donated flowers?"

"We've lined their coffers every other year before this. They may as well do something for us. A wreath, really. It's the least they could do. If you'd like, I can make the call. Hanson's on State Street. You're not related, are you?"

Aya had often gotten that question growing up but never in the process of begging for flowers.

"I think we share a great-grandfather or something," she said. "My aunt Jessie would know. I'm not big on genealogy."

Mrs. Irving peered at her. "Pity. Well, I'll tell them it's for their cousin. That ought to shame them into giving us something."

"Mrs. Irving, please. I don't think the museum is really in the position to be asking for favors."

"Nonsense," said the tall, willowy woman, leaning so she could read Aya's computer screen. Aya snapped it shut.

"If that's all," she said, but of course it wasn't.

"The festival," said Mrs. Irving sharply. "Rumors are flying. I would have talked to Noah Kato myself, of course, only he wasn't home when I went in yesterday. And his parents weren't giving away his whereabouts, which is not like them."

Aya tried not to smile. At least she was in on one conspiracy.

"Probably back in California, going out with more of those actress-model types," Mrs. Irving said primly. "It's very disappointing. I know his parents worried for him! His mother practically raised him on feminist theory, yet there he was, in the tabloids every other week with another lady. Doing nothing but making those albums, and what did he do with the rest of his time, I would like to know."

Aya made an effort to appear cheerful. "I guess he was busy."

Mrs. Irving was certainly the type of woman who would make albums in her spare hours while holding down at least one and half difficult, meaningful jobs, and she sniffed. "Well, he certainly seemed too busy to visit. And with all his sister went through. It's a disgrace."

Aya blinked. She thought that she remembered Twyla starting to say something about Nami then changing the subject after a look from their mother. They were not allowed to gossip. It was a household rule, the like of which she never seemed to encounter in anyone else's house. They could share others' good news, but that was it.

Mrs. Irving was not at all bothered by Aya's lack of

response. "I found his office. Girl named Grace, more efficient than I would have expected. She was vague about details, though. I presented her with a list of our demands."

"Mrs. Irving," Aya finally managed, "I'm not sure we're in a position to be making demands. The festival is bringing in ten thousand people. We only have three hundred."

"Yes," said Mrs. Irving. "And what is their festival all about? They don't even have a proper theme."

"Okay," said Aya. "Tell me what you would like the festival to do."

Mrs. Irving reached into her handbag and brought out a list that was several pages long, much more detailed and unreasonable than any of Aya's requests.

"No music at all on the second day, at least not until after eight in the evening? Donations of all unsold food at the end of each day, plus complimentary T-shirts for everyone? There's no way they'll agree to this."

"Well," said Mrs. Irving, "between you, me, and the fence post, they do seem rather strapped for funds. But with ten thousand attendees, that will be their own fault. I would have managed things much better."

It was an incredibly arrogant statement, but it was also probably true.

"I need to run home for a bit," said Aya. It was clearly going to be the only way to get Mrs. Irving to leave. "But I'll give these to Noah Kato myself."

"Is he back in town?" she asked.

Aya flinched. "I'm not sure. But I can get in touch with him if needed."

Mrs. Irving harrumphed as they walked out together. "Technology," she said. "You young people. You may never learn that the most effective way to do business is face-to-face."

Mrs. Irving, thought Aya, *if nothing else, I've certainly learned that from you.*

40

Noah

He approached Aya's house with a heart full of confidence. Perhaps he didn't deserve it, but he had never before felt so sure about her affection. After all, people who didn't like you didn't show the level of passion she had. Heck, there had been women who were genuinely interested in him over the years, but because he never let things progress too far, they had never been allowed to prove it.

Noah had truly thought he knew everything there was to know. After all, even if he didn't have direct experience, he wasn't an obedient-enough Catholic to stop himself from thinking about it. It had been such a relief when he decided he didn't have to submit to those teachings anymore, which had not so coincidentally happened around the time one of his friends came out, years before Nobu. At the time, Noah insisted that if Drew wasn't going to theology classes anymore, he wouldn't go either, and his parents acquiesced fairly easily.

Also, the basics were pretty clear to Noah too. After all,

he didn't exactly live under a rock. And he'd been happy, over the years, to join in the laugher when jokes like "Calculus is the missionary position of math" were bandied around. As long as you laughed just enough, nobody would ever guess you were lying.

But it turned out that "virgin" had been the perfect word to describe him. Because he could never have imagined the intense combination of lust, longing, and trust that had made his night—and morning—with Aya so explosive. It had been much better than he would have imagined.

Noah had parked a block down from the house. He'd borrowed his mom's car, but he still didn't want any rumors to start. As he came closer, he saw that Emi was on the porch, rocking on the porch swing. She was talking on the phone, frowning. He raised a hand in greeting, and she gave a fleeting smile.

"I know," she said quietly. "But because of the baby, I'm just saying that may have to change."

Noah drew a breath. How strange that Emi was going to have a baby. He could still hardly believe Hana was his niece. It made him feel young somehow—irresponsible. Sure, he had a house in LA that would be considered a mansion by Love Hollow standards—though not by LA standards, of course. He had his own car, though it was back in the garage, and more kitchen gadgets than he could ever figure out how to use. But he also had no degree, no family members out in California with him, and no paycheck.

Of course, now he had a girlfriend—or something. Hoping to give Emi a little privacy for her phone conversation, he knocked on the door.

Aya answered, but it took her a moment. And when she showed him in, her smile was cautious.

"Hi," she said, closing the door behind her.

He drew her in, and once he started kissing her, he felt the chaos of the morning evaporating. He turned her around, and soon, he was pressing her against the door, touching every part of her body.

A knock sounded at the door, and they startled as they broke apart.

"Sorry," said Emi, grinning a bit as she came in. She had put her phone away. "Just needed to pee for, you know, like the millionth time today."

"Is something wrong?" asked Aya.

"Relax, *Mom*," said Emi. "It's normal at this stage. It just means I'm sufficiently hydrated. Also, we need to go get some more snacks later. Your mom is way too health conscious. I've picked this place clean."

"Okay," said Aya. She was pink, not looking at Noah. "Um, Noah, do you want some tea?"

"Sure."

Though Emi didn't emerge again after going upstairs, her presence changed things. As much as Noah wanted to keep kissing Aya, he did have some decorum. After all, it wasn't even Aya's house. It was the place where Noah was always expected to be on his best behavior, and he still felt that he might be scolded if he so much as rumpled a seat cushion.

"How are you doing?" he asked.

Aya was filling the kettle. "Fine," she said. "And you?"

"Not bad," he managed. "It's a little cramped at my parents'."

"That's right," she said, pursing her lips. "You have a lot more space in California, I'm sure."

"Yes," he said, smiling. "A little too much. Or a lot too much, really. I end up just rattling around in those rooms."

She nodded briskly. "Well, count your blessings. I'm

probably going to have to find a roommate when I go back to Chicago. No rattling around there, not on a graduate stipend."

"What about the museum?" he asked—too quickly, he realized, so he tried to change the question. "Would you ever consider moving away from Chicago?"

"Both of my jobs require me to basically live on-site, so unless I win the lottery, I very much doubt it," she said curtly. "I have to live near one of them. We don't have anything to eat with this tea. Emi ate all the snacks."

"I guess she needs them," he said. "Or the baby does."

Finally, Aya smiled. "Yes, the baby is already making demands. Which is good, because Charles seems to have plenty of his own demands."

"I haven't met him," said Noah.

Aya shook her head. "Neither have I. He's coming out here soon, though. Emi didn't want to cut her visit short just because of the news."

Noah swallowed. "So," he said. "I talked to Grace."

Aya came closer. "Okay. Tell me now, I guess. Let's get it over with."

She had so much anguish in her face that Noah just wanted to hold her. But he snuck a look at the empty rooms around them. *What if another Hanson family member bursts in on us?*

"Can we go up to your room?" he murmured, taking her hand.

Aya took her hand away. "Did you hear what I was telling you?" she said. "It is. Not. A good time."

He recoiled. Because he'd never let himself get close to anyone, he'd also not experienced a lot of rejection. And it stung bitterly. He found himself wanting to head over to the mirror in the hall to see if he looked okay. *Should I have shaved? Is that it? Do I look bad?* Of course, it didn't really matter how he looked. He would never be as attractive as Aya. Maybe he was just a typical idiot, trying to use his money and status to date someone well out of his league. Maybe that was why old, ugly guys in show business ended up with young models. They knew they would never be able to compete with successful women their own age, but at least with women who were young and semi-anonymous, there might be some semblance of parity.

Of course, things didn't usually go well for those guys either.

Emi chose that moment to come back down. "Aya, did you still want help with the programs? Because I think I figured out a couple of ways to get them to look better in black and white."

"Why not sepia?" asked Noah. He remembered the thick programs for Pilgrimages in years past, particularly because he was often bored during the ceremony as a kid. It was fascinating to look at the glossy portraits and the lists of names.

"Can't afford it," said Aya shortly. "Sure, Emi. Let's head out."

Noah followed them, wondering if they would invite him.

Eventually, as they were getting in the car, Emi remembered. "I'm sorry, Noah. Do you want to come with us?"

He looked at Aya, but she was staring straight ahead.

"Um, n-no, that's fine," he said quickly. "See you later."

41

———————

Noah

Noah's head was reeling. "Why would they tell Arkanyon Products to back out? Is there some sort of corporate conspiracy?"

Grace rolled her eyes. "Well, apparently, corporations are people, so I'm not sure that 'conspiracy' is the way we're allowed to describe agreements between them. Even the illegal ones."

"Seriously, though," he said. "Why do you think they would say something to Arkanyon? Won't this festival at least get a few people listening to my music, making them more money?"

"They must have heard a rumor about you trying to poach one of their biggest assets. Did you tell anyone about Evie?"

"Of course not!" he snapped. "But she's so unhappy. Isn't it obvious she's thinking of leaving?"

Grace adjusted her headband. "I can't be sure. A lot of recording artists are unhappy. That doesn't necessarily mean they'll jump ship."

"Well, it's stupid of them not to." He amended it immediately. "I mean, strange of them not to but fine."

"Everyone wants to make a living," Grace said. "Speaking of which, our balance sheet is not balancing now. So for all our sakes, you'll need to help us out of this. The core staff start tomorrow, and we have to make payroll."

"Okay," he said. "Well, we'll just have to cut a few corners."

Grace held his gaze. "You don't really seem to be getting this, do you? Arkanyon was one of our biggest sponsors."

He shrugged. "Can we get other sponsors?"

Grace sighed. "Don't you think I've been trying? This is the eleventh hour, Noah. Even a well-worded request for money for a festival that's about to start is not necessarily going over well."

"What else can we do?"

She patted the swivel chair next to her. Noah hated those chairs, though he tried to settle in next to Grace. He preferred to sit on a cushion on the floor, laptop on the coffee table his mother had brought by, looking for solutions to problems.

Except it seemed they were out of the easy solutions.

"There's not much left," she said quietly. "And, Noah, I'm sorry, but I can't go without a paycheck."

He put a hand to his mouth. "God, Grace, you know I would never ask you to do that!"

"I know you would never *ask*," she said. "But the thing is, Noah, when there's not an account from which I can be paid? It amounts to the same thing."

"I'll sell something," he said. "My car."

"How? You're not there to sell it. You know it's not going to go for the same price you got it for, don't you?"

"My parents always told me never to buy a new c-car," he mumbled.

Grace nodded, solemn. "Well, they're probably right about that. And how are you going to accomplish this sale?"

"Ask your friend, the one with that weird Mohawk. Isn't she always looking for work?"

Grace looked at him quizzically. "Thea? You know, that's not a bad idea."

"Not all my ideas are bad," he said and finally got a small smile out of her.

"Okay, so we'll use the money from the sale of your car, minus whatever we pay Thea," Grace said. Noah could see her tallying figures in her head. "That's about a third of what we need. We still need about a hundred thousand dollars. What else should we do?"

"I don't know. But I'll find something. Okay?"

Grace looked skeptical. "It might be more efficient, at this point, to cancel," she said. "Then at least we won't end up having to pay the full amount."

"There is no we. You'll get paid, right? And the staff who are coming tomorrow?"

"For as long as the car money lasts, yes," she said.

"Then that's where we are now. Now, I'm going to make some calls."

"Really?" Grace perked up. One of her perpetual complaints was that Noah was overreliant on email, even when calling would be more effective. Since Grace was also young, he couldn't claim it was generational. He just hated having a stutter to contend with.

"No," he said. "But I'm going to send a lot of emails. There's got to be someone who would love this kind of advertising."

"Yes, but are they prepared to pay a hundred grand for it?"

Noah pretended not to hear.

"I'm leaving the museum stuff to you," he said. "Can you handle it?"

"I *could*," said Grace. "But I consider it your mess."

"Mess?"

"Whatever you want to call it," she said, turning back to her work. "You and your friend Aya need to figure it out. I wouldn't want to get in the way of that."

42

Aya

Aya ended up at her mother's studio. She hadn't meant to go there. There was no escape from the number of things she needed to complete at the museum. But eventually, Emi dragged her out.

"I haven't gotten what I needed," Aya moaned on her way out the door. The sunset, she noticed rather abruptly, was beautiful. The night before, she had been able to appreciate the sight. But now it just heralded her doom. *If the sun is almost setting and I've made virtually no progress, what does that mean?* She should really stay up all night, working on both her doctorate and the Pilgrimage, if she was going to make a go of either.

"Yes, but I need to eat," said Emi patiently. "Unless you want me to faint."

"You probably have trail mix in your bag," Aya grumbled. Emi was a master of preparation.

"You don't know that," Emi said patiently.

Her mom was between classes. She was in the little

storage closet that functioned as a makeshift office, balancing the books. Aya envied her mother's abilities. *How did she run a business while raising three daughters?* Aya had been tasked with one thing, saving the museum, and even that had been beyond her abilities. Their balance sheet looked terrible. At least they were not likely to lose the building during the Pilgrimage itself, though she wondered what would happen immediately after.

"Good evening," said Emi cheerfully. "Any luck on the bathroom situation?"

Aya's mother pulled her in for a quick hug. "Nothing on my end, I'm afraid. But I am good at rounding up volunteers. Aya, would you like someone else to take on a day or two of the Pilgrimage? Twyla said Professor Jin may need you during that time. Really, it's no trouble."

Aya pulled away, horrified. "Mom, the Pilgrimage is the one part of my job that usually goes well! That's the most important thing I do all year! You would really want to take me away from that?"

"I just thought you might need help with it," her mother murmured. "I know there's been too much on your shoulders, Aya. I'm afraid I gave you too much responsibility when you were younger. I've always felt that—"

"That I can't handle anything? Thanks for the vote of confidence. We were going to see if you wanted dinner, but I think we'll just go."

She saw Emi mouthing an apology, which annoyed her more. And she heard a familiar voice coming over from next to the barre.

"Are you ready to start?"

She poked her head around the doorway.

"Oh, hi," said Twyla, exchanging glances with their

mother. And Aya noticed her mother and Twyla were dressed identically. Instead of the casual skirts that had to be tied on, they were wearing floaty black skirts. And instead of ballet pink, which was usually the color of choice, they were both in black leotards.

"What is this?" asked Aya.

But there was no response.

She looked at the two of them. Their other sister, Martha, would probably have been part of this, except thank goodness, her work was keeping her in Japan for the time being. That was more or less how Aya's childhood had been. Mom, Twyla, and Martha on one side, united by their love of dance and their ballerina bodies, and Aya on the other side, too large to look good in half the costumes.

She had also asked her mother if she could be in a pageant. There was one that would have been perfect, and from the age of six, Aya had always asked to participate. Little Miss Love Hollow would have been ideal. They wouldn't have even needed to travel, and at that age, Aya had already started singing lessons, so she had an obvious act for the talent portion. She could have even combined singing and dancing, if her mom would let her.

But her parents had both denied her that opportunity. And years later, Aya was forced to watch from the sidelines as Twyla and Martha alternated year after year. If one of them won Little Miss Love Hollow, that was a virtual guarantee that the other one would win the next year. So it was no surprise that they both ended up winning Miss Love Hollow, too, and becoming finalists for Miss Idaho.

Half the time, Aya wasn't even allowed to watch.

"Fine," she snapped. "You can just stay. I'll figure this out. But no, Mom, I don't need you to do my job for me."

"Aya..." Twyla was getting close, probably trying to go in for some sort of conciliatory hug.

"No," said Aya. "I get it."

And she walked out.

43

———

Noah

He thought about texting Aya that night. But he didn't because she had been so accusatory at her mom's house. He wondered whether that was just her personality. Perhaps she, like other enlightened women of her generation, had decided to treat her lovers with the same wry indifference that men had made use of for centuries.

Aya actually didn't seem very much like the one he had once known. She'd had few friends, but the people close to her were treated like royalty. But she must have changed in the intervening years. She had probably expected him to change too.

Noah woke in the morning resolute. At the very least, their night—and morning—together had been good. Mind-blowingly so, in fact, and he knew that there was no way it had all been fake. So if nothing else, she would probably be willing to see him again just for that.

He only needed to figure out how to ask her out on a date. They had to be out of public view, and they needed somewhere to go after. Not a hotel, because those were all booked, and not their parents' houses. Pickings were slim, especially since the cabin was going to be otherwise occupied.

Nobu had reminded him of it early that morning, waking him up with a ruthlessness only a sibling could possess.

"Hello," he said. "My darling brother, stop being laaazy."

Noah pulled the pillow over his head. "Stop. I don't have to go in until nine."

"Early to bed, early to rise," said Nobu. "What? You would strand your brother on the day he needs the most help? Rude!"

Noah sighed. "Fine. I can help you. I just have to go into the office after."

His eyes were so dry that the clock next to him was blurry, but the shapes eventually formed into numbers— 6:45 a.m.

"Great," said Nobu loudly. "You are here to help by cooking breakfast. Thank you!"

He headed out just as Justin, his fiancé, was coming in.

"Jackass," said Justin, shaking his head at Nobu. But there was only resignation in his tone, not anger. He smiled down at Noah.

"Sorry, man. I told him not to wake you up. But he couldn't resist."

"It's fine. I assume breakfast has already been cooked?"

Justin laughed. "That would be correct. Seems you Katos don't like going hungry."

Noah rubbed his eyes. "Great. But let me know if you need help with anything, okay?"

"Just come to the party tomorrow," said Justin. "And you know, plus-ones are welcome."

Noah raised his eyebrows. "Word travels fast, huh?"

Justin, who was from Denver, grinned. "I guess so. I don't know much about small towns, but at least in Love Hollow, the gossip seems to pass from person to person pretty much instantly."

Noah smiled. "Okay, well, probably, everyone else knows more than I do at this point."

Silence followed. Noah was thankful that his brother wasn't in the room anymore. Nobu would have pressed him. He'd always been a good judge of character, and Noah had relied on his opinions for as long as he could remember. When he'd been bullied in middle school for being too into music and other "girl" stuff, Nobu was the one who taught him how to defend himself, both physically and with cutting remarks. He'd also seen to it that Noah made a wider group of friends, which helped him guard against bullying after that. Nobu always had a sharp eye, and he could instantly pick out the kids like Bobby L., the ones who only valued popularity.

"Is your family doing okay?" asked Noah. "What do they think about Love Hollow?"

Justin shrugged. "For my mom, it's probably rugged. And sort of exotic, you know? Her kind of thing, at least for a week. My dad and stepmom, I'm not sure about."

"And you have a sister, right?"

He thought he remembered that the dad and stepmom had a kid together.

"Yeah, but she's in high school. So you know, everything is very uncool as far as she's concerned."

"Well, they picked a great time of year to visit."

Justin started to smile. He looked a bit like their dad when he got that expression on his face, a small smile that was easy to miss. Noah wondered if his brother had been attracted to that somehow, if there was a cliché about gay men marrying guys who reminded them of their fathers. Justin was definitely the calm that balanced Nobu's fiery personality, so in that that sense, he was similar to their dad too.

"I mean, we planned the party at this time because of the festival," he said. "So it's not really a coincidence that it's your favorite time of year."

Noah was surprised. "I hate to say it, dude, but does Nobu know he's going to hate pretty much everything that's there? We have approximately zero classical acts."

"Oh, he knows," said Justin, grinning. "But he really wanted you to be able to come to the party."

Noah frowned. "I make my own schedule. I could've come anytime."

Pausing, Justin shifted slightly. "Look, I don't doubt it. But sometimes things come up, you know? They get in the way."

"Like what?" said Noah.

Justin shook his head. "I really don't know anything about your industry." "Between Nobu and me, all we have is the middle school world and the public library world. But it seems like there are studio things. Meetings. Tours."

"Oh, well, of course I can't interrupt a tour," said Noah, his annoyance rising. His family, for some reason, always wanted him to visit when he was in the middle of a series of tour dates that had been booked a year earlier. They regarded it as some sort of insane slight that he couldn't take a last-minute vacation.

Justin edged toward the door. "Sure," he said. "You know, stuff like that."

44

N oah
Noah took his time preparing for the day. Back in California, he had learned a sixteen-step skin regimen popularized by the viral video "Sixteen Steps to Sweet, Sweet Skin," which featured a D-list actress dancing around her bathroom with a plethora of expensive products. Unfortunately, Noah was smack-dab in the target audience, as he had an income that allowed him to buy all sixteen plus a need to maintain that income by looking good.

The first day back home, Nami had seen him trying to organize all of his products while not missing a step in the extensive routine. She started laughing so hard she peed her pants. Since then, he had tried to do it covertly, but it was hard when he had to use the hall bathroom and anyone who was awake would notice what he was doing. And that night with Aya, he had completely missed the routine, yet his skin had been glowing the next day.

So he snuck into the hall bathroom. The least he could do was shave and moisturize. It made him feel ever so slightly ready to face the day. While he scrutinized his skin under the yellow, unflattering light, he thought about what Justin had been saying. He would definitely have come to the engagement party. He would have considered it unmissable.

While he was looking for a softer towel, the memory of Nami's gender reveal party came back to him. His mother had yanked the phone away from his dad. Even though he couldn't see it, he could picture the exchange.

"I don't like gender reveal parties," Noah said. "Look, I've been to enough out here. They're universally tacky."

"Yes, that is exactly the point, Noah," his mom told him. "Whether you are personally fond of the exact variety of party. And if you are not, there is no way you should even consider making the trip."

"Great," he told her, clicking through his email. "I've got a photo shoot that weekend anyway."

The party, of course, seemed like great fun. Nami had some amazing friends from high school, so they were there. Two of her closest friends were Twyla and Martha, Aya's little sisters. Aya had been there, too, though she wasn't in many of the photos. Noah had decided it really was the whole weird "gender reveal" thing that had kept him away. But if he had been willing to be honest with his family, he might have admitted that the thought of seeing Aya was overwhelming. *Would we talk? Pretend to be casual? Try to avoid each other?* It seemed like way too many decisions to have to make in the space of a short little party, decisions he'd been happy to avoid at the time.

After fixing his part in the mirror, he gave a wry smile. Maybe if he had only seen Aya, they would have gotten back together a lot sooner. If that had happened, the weekend would have been taxing but not in the way he expected.

When he got in the kitchen, Nobu and Justin were preparing to leave.

"Dad needs you to go move some furniture for the nice lady next door!" Nobu sang. His voice was still way too loud, and Noah winced.

"Why?" he mumbled.

"Bye," said Nobu. "Enjoy your indentured servitude, dear brother! It's long overdue!"

Justin stopped to give hugs to everyone before he departed. He stroked Nami's hair. Apparently, the whole Kato family was gathering at the break of dawn.

"You don't have to go yet, of course," said Noah's mother. "Stacy texted me, and I said I'd send you over later."

"I'm not going to go help her," said Noah.

"Then you'll be forcing your father to go with his bad back. I hope you've thought that one through."

"I can't believe you're going over!" said Noah. "For what? She's trying to close the museum."

"She's not trying very hard, Noah," said his father. "She was never the ringleader."

Noah opened the fridge then closed it. He was so used to spending time with people who avoided carbs that it still felt strange to have a normal breakfast. He took out everything his parents had made—miso soup, rice, fried mushrooms, oatmeal with berries. There had apparently been bacon, but Nobu had clearly finished it off. Only the wonderful aroma remained.

When he was seated, he glared at his parents. "Tell me the story," he said. "Then I'll decide if I want to join."

His parents told it in fits and starts. It had all started with a so-called "society" of people who voiced their loud opinions at school board meetings. They had all kinds of changes they wanted to see at the school, of course, and at first, it was just a loose collection of issues. But they soon began to concentrate on one specific thing. Field trips and research with the Internment Memorial Museum had always been part of Love Hollow High's history curriculum. And it made things interesting for the students. More than one graduate had come back reporting that they were much more comfortable with primary source research than their college classmates. The combination of digital database access, well-maintained archives, and original research was a boon for the seniors who took the advanced American History course each year.

That was, until the society people turned against the projects.

Their leader, Carl, always had a mustache and a scowl. He had worked for his father's real estate company for his entire working life, so unfortunately, he had both disposable income and lots of free time. And he seemed intent on devoting all of it to blocking access to Love Hollow's biggest museum. All at once, all the schools were barred from having field trips there. The partnerships between the museum and local businesses broke down one by one. Carl didn't mind tourism, but he was determined that nobody should visit the museum. Any tourist who looked the least bit Asian was going to be scrutinized, even if they had just come for mountain biking in the hills, not a museum visit.

Carl's argument seemed to be that the students weren't learning "the good things" about America anymore. It was rather strange, as he was only in his early fifties, so he hadn't exactly grown up in an era where America was overly romanticized. He wanted any talk of World War II to begin and end with acts of heroism in Europe, and he would have happily skipped over the entire Vietnam War— except to disagree with pardons for draft dodgers. He seemed to have a strange focus on the Battle of Little Bighorn, which to him, epitomized American heroism. He viewed with great skepticism and hostility anyone who said a word about "Indians." "Native American" wasn't in his vocabulary, much less "Indigenous peoples" or "First Tribes."

Few of Carl's followers were quite as bombastic as he was, but it didn't matter. They'd done their damage. The *Love Hollow Gazette* was filled with warring letters to the editor, and the high school history teacher ended up resigning and taking a job in Oregon instead. The Katos had to step down from the museum's board, as they were accused of having a conflict of interest. They'd even stayed away from museum events, although they still attended the Pilgrimage every year.

"We blend in there," joked Noah's dad. "If anyone says they saw me, I'll just tell them it was actually someone else. And they'll probably believe that."

Noah's mother shook her head. She was clearly not ready to joke about the matter.

"Mom, why are you even still here? I had no idea it had gotten this horrible."

She raised her eyebrows. "And go where, Noah? Some antiracist la-la land where we wouldn't encounter anything like this?"

He stayed quiet for a moment. "Maybe a place where, you know, there are more Asian people?"

She smiled. "We would be abandoning the people who are here. Even Aya's family. How would you feel about that?"

He didn't have an answer. Though his heart sang that Aya was going to move away, that she would come to his house in LA and bring the homey quality it had never held for him, he wasn't ready to say that. In fact, Aya had seemed extremely unwilling to consider a move to California. But perhaps he hadn't done enough to convince her.

His father put his hands on the table and rose more slowly than Noah remembered. "Anyway," he said. "One of us had better go over and move that end table."

Noah stood, but he wasn't admitting defeat quite yet. "After everything you told me? How about she calls her friend Carl and has him move it for her?"

His mother smiled tightly. "Oh, she doesn't actually think much of Carl. None of them do."

His father seemed to see that his approach wasn't working. "She's our neighbor, Noah."

"Don't make this a Catholic thing. Love thy neighbor, blah blah blah."

"Fine, then. I won't. But if we refuse to help her, who benefits? She'll think we're bad neighbors, and let's face it, we will be. She'll also be even less likely to consider our perspective in the future."

"But you don't even challenge her," he said. "She's charged with teaching children! How is this good for them?"

"Having no teachers isn't great for them, Noah," his father said sternly. "Do you know how hard it is for us to find permanent teachers, even substitutes? We always have vacancies. We had to fill the high school history position with a recent grad, and after what she endured this past year, she quit. I'm surprised she lasted the whole school year, honestly."

His mother's mouth was firmly set. "Your father refuses to force any of the other teachers to transfer into that position."

"They would leave too," he said quietly, touching his wife's arm. "So I'd be losing even more teachers. What would be the point of that?"

Noah was with his mother. "You should force the teachers who agree with this shit to take those vacancies."

His dad started to smile again. "And have our high schoolers taught by someone who thinks that the internment was not a problem, perhaps even a brilliant idea? Oh, I don't think so. I'd take the position myself before that happened."

"Well, you may have to," said his wife. "You're not going to find anyone else to do it. And our students can't graduate or go out into the world with no knowledge of history. Unlike their parents."

At that point in the conversation, Nami chose to come in. "You could change it all, Noah."

Their mother, seeing where her thoughts were going, made to hush her. "It's not his responsibility."

But Nami wasn't listening. With Hana asleep in her arms, she said quietly but fiercely, "Then whose responsibility is it, Mom? If our family doesn't do something, who will?"

"Why d-don't..." Noah began, but his stutter prevented him from getting the rest of the sentence out.

"Don't you dare ask me to pay for it," snapped Nami. "Don't you think I would if I possibly could, a hundred times over? Don't you think I hate having to fight Byron for child support?"

It was the first time she had mentioned her ex—the first time Noah had heard his name since he'd been back, actually. Even when he was alone with his parents, they seemed to be perfectly willing to pretend he was dead.

"Nami," said their father. "Sweetheart. You don't have to fight him. If it's better for you to drop the rope—"

"It's *not* better for me," she hissed. Her scowl was at odds with the gentle movements she was making to keep her daughter asleep. Back and forth, back and forth, she rocked her. But her eyes were bright with hatred. "That bastard needs to pay."

"I agree," said their mother, muttering a word in Japanese that she usually reserved for the worst men she had ever encountered. Noah almost never heard her use the word, but she and Nami seemed united in their anger.

"I was going to ask if there were any fundraising avenues that were, you know, untapped," he offered weakly.

His mother shook her head, ushering Nami out with Hana.

His father took over the discussion. "Your Aya..."

Noah shook his head. "She's not m-mine dad, not in any way. She's not even answering my texts right now."

"Your Aya," he said, that time with a slight smile, "she really did the best she could. The museum got all kinds of grants. There were lots of fundraisers. Everyone who had ever visited was asked to contribute. But without visitors and without community support? It's been an uphill battle."

"So what's going to happen?"

His father shrugged. "Housing costs are going up," he said carefully. "And the land it's on is very valuable. So it'll likely be sold to pay off debts."

"But the main building itself could stay open, right?"

His father gave a sad smile. "Noah, you have a fancy house. Do you really think you would want to share it with a museum? One that reminds everyone that this is just a place, one with a dark past, not some sort of Western paradise?"

Noah felt another jolt of guilt at his father's words. "My house isn't that fancy," he said. "Not for the neighborhood. Not for LA, really. It's just that I needed something private—"

His father waved a hand. "It's okay, Noah," he said. "You give what you can."

Noah squirmed. He hadn't been giving, not really. He went to fancy charity galas, sure, the ones with the best canapés and the highest chance of being photographed with beautiful women. What a waste all that had been, he reflected. He should have just written checks instead. And he should never have forgotten Love Hollow. In the days when he'd had more cash, he could have made sizable contributions, maybe even kept the museum from floundering. Now, when they most needed his help, he couldn't open his wallet.

45

Aya

Of course Noah Kato thought he could just show up at the museum, expecting a tour. Aya pulled her hair back, walking briskly to the door to let him in.

"My dad told me what happened," he said without preamble. "I w-wanted to come and see the museum. And there was something I wanted to ask you about too. I feel b-bad for missing the Pilgrimage this year."

"If you wanted to come, you shouldn't have scheduled a festival that's going to take place at the exact same time."

He nodded vigorously. "I know. I'm terrible at scheduling. Justin was just telling me that."

She frowned. "Nobu's fiancé? Is he here?"

"Yes," he said then he started speaking quickly. "And he told me I should take you to their engagement party tomorrow afternoon. I mean, if you want to come. As my date. You don't have to. But Justin asked, so I mean, I guess I need to tell him?"

A little bubble of happiness welling up inside Aya. She tried to stop it, of course, telling herself she wasn't even really being invited by Noah. She was being asked by Justin. And probably just because he felt sorry for Noah. But Aya had always liked Nobu, and she missed the Kato family.

"Of course," she said. "Tell them I'll be there."

She looked around the museum. Beyond the entrance, one large gallery was open to the public. The archives were in a separate room, and there was a reading room too.

Her back became straighter. In spite of the lack of finances, she was proud of her work at the museum. And Noah deserved to see just what he had neglected when he let stardom go to his head.

"We can start with the gallery," Aya said. "We have one of our best exhibitions out. We were really lucky to get this in time for the Pilgrimage."

The exhibit was fantastic. Noah said he had expected the museum to have just one set of material on display all the time.

Aya shook her head. "It's dynamic," she explained. "As the director, I really wanted to focus on collaborating with other institutions. So we loaned a bunch of things to the Civil Rights Museum for one of their displays, and they gave us these artifacts. We shared a lot of designs beforehand, of course, so we could make it fit together."

As Noah walked around, examining the exhibit, he whistled. "This is amazing. I've n-never seen something like this before."

Aya didn't explain the background of the exhibit, though she wondered if he might be able to guess. Thanks to Carl, the town's resident antimuseum crusader, there had been a lot of accusations that they were "playing up" a rare, ugly facet of American life during the Second World War. Apparently, everything else was fine and dandy, and any individual who didn't land in an internment camp was either fighting Hitler in Europe or living a full, happy life. Aya had designed and gotten funding for an exhibit showing what life was life in Memphis and Love Hollow during one particular year, 1943. Alongside pictures of Japanese American families with suitcases and strained expressions, there were Whites Only signs on lunch counters and news articles about lynchings. Young men of every color were dying in Europe then coming home to a violent, segregated society.

Of course, Carl would never get near the exhibit. He was a person who would probably say that the centuries-long suffering of any group of people was not a big deal.

Aya tried to forget about Carl for a moment. "I'm glad you like it," she said, sighing. "It might be our last exhibit for a while. Or maybe ever."

One donation from Noah could change the entire course of the museum. All they really needed was a small one. Okay, maybe two hundred thousand dollars, enough to fund part of the renovations and pay one staff member.

And Aya wasn't willing to admit that the donation controlled something else too. It controlled her life. If the museum were funded, she would be able to leave, carrying only her guilt with her. She could go finish her PhD without worrying that the place would crumble, even if she would still feel bad for not finishing everything she'd meant to do. At the moment, as hard as she was working, she wasn't going to have much of a choice. She couldn't just let the museum sit unattended for a year, not allowing visitors. It would mean the death of the only institution in Love Hollow interested in preserving the town's history.

Noah sighed. "I'm sorry it's been such a tough time."

Aya tried to shove down her disappointment. "It hasn't been that tough. I mean, our grandparents were in an internment camp when they were younger than we are now. And I'm reminded of that every day."

"They wouldn't have wanted to see this happening, though."

"I'm glad they didn't," Aya snapped. "If some of these people in Love Hollow had to answer to folks who were actually here, they might think about it all differently."

"Some of the people coming for the Pilgrimage were interned here, right?"

She nodded. "Sure. But the last thing I want to do to the nonagenarians is force them to confront our local dickheads. No need to add any new trauma."

After an uncomfortable silence, she beckoned to Noah. "Come on. Let's go to the reading room. At least it has a good view."

The landscape would have been desolate, but the temporary employees were buzzing around the festival grounds. It was the first sound check, so a random group of people were singing into microphones, banging on drum sets, and playing electric guitars. They were really good, actually. Music festivals always seemed to attract offbeat people who were talented musicians, so Aya wasn't shocked.

"Aya," Noah said, turning away from the window. "I don't know how to fix this. But it's not because I don't care about you."

"How am I supposed to know that?" she asked, another tear streaking down her cheek. She held her head up, but the tears kept coming down, whether she wanted them to or not.

"Trust me," he said and kissed her.

Aya did not feel her body melt. She was still angry. Furious, in fact.

But she couldn't keep herself from kissing Noah back. It wasn't a contradiction, not exactly. Just something that she couldn't help doing.

The music had stopped, thank God.

46
———————

Aya

Emi was helping Aya get ready for the party, just like in high school, in a way. Except back then, they hadn't been invited to many parties. Sheena's parents had let her throw a New Year's Eve party once. But the dumpling kids ended up hiding out in Sheena's bedroom, escaping the orange peel game that the "cooler" invitees were playing downstairs. From then on, they had decided they would spend each New Year's with one another.

"You look gorgeous," said Emi. "You're glowing."

Aya rolled her eyes. "I'm sorry, preggo. Aren't you the one who's supposed to be glowing?"

Emi touched her neck. "I'm feeling kind of sick, actually. I think I might just stay here."

"Stop. I'm sure the cabin will be cozy. You can just, like, take a nap or something."

Aya's dress was a pale-peach color, the kind that would be considered "skin tone" for the average American white woman. But because Aya's skin was darker than the dress, it made for some contrast. It had long sleeves and a huge tea-length skirt with more tulle than she ever would have worn ordinarily. But she had to be fancy without shopping, so it was as good as it was going to get. She'd bought it to wear to a formal university event years ago, but at the last minute, she'd caved and worn a nondescript black dress instead. It had taken Twyla and Emi all morning to persuade her to wear it instead of jeans.

"Gay men are going to take it as an insult if you wear jeans to a formal engagement party," said Twyla. "I mean, the invitation specified Japanese formal or American cocktail, so unless you want Mom busting out one of her old kimonos, you're going to wear this."

The memory of the Kato yukata made Aya blush. "Fine," she told her sister, and Twyla flounced off with a smirk. Aya hadn't even asked how Twy had known what was on the invitation. Aya hadn't received a physical invitation, but if Justin was expecting her, she wasn't going to skip it.

Though she was sorely tempted.

Emi smiled, stretching herself out on Aya's bed. "Yes, I'm sure Nobu and Justin care so little about their engagement party that they're ready to let people literally sleep through it."

"Or nap in the car. Whatever you want."

Emi shook her head. "That's the part I don't like. I think even driving over there is going to make me queasy. Good thing they didn't do it up at the cabin."

Aya stared at her. "But it *is* at the cabin. They've been getting the place ready for weeks!"

"Apparently, the weather's too dicey. According to Twyla, anyway. They're doing it at the Katos' house."

"How does Twyla know all this?" grumbled Aya, digging through her vanity for a bobby pin.

"She would say she has her sources." Emi let another little smile flit across her face.

Aya glanced up at the mirror, shooting Emi a look. "You're enjoying this, aren't you."

Emi grinned. "I have to admit I really am. Though I'm sad my parents are on vacation. They could have been my spies at this shindig."

"Oh, what do you need spies for?" Aya went over to her closet to find some suitable shoes. If she could just find some ballet-style black shoes, that was as fancy as she was going to be able to get. Wearing heels would bring her slightly closer to Noah's height but at the rather steep cost of rendering her unable to walk.

"What do you think of these?" she asked Emi, waving around some maroon flats that had seen better days.

Emi wrinkled her nose. "Might as well go in your tennis shoes."

Aya knew she would be expected to ditch her shoes at the door in the Kato house, as she had always done at her own house. They weren't a critical part of the outfit.

"Oh, hush," she said, slipping her foot into one of the shoes. At least they still fit. "I won't even have to wear them for very long."

"Wear what?" Twyla asked, poking her head in the door just as she had always done when Aya was younger and no less annoying. "Your clothes?"

Aya held the shoe up, ready to throw it, but Twyla had already flounced off.

"Seriously, though," said Emi. "What's up with you guys?"

"Well, he's a celebrity. I'm not. He's rich. I'm not."

"But?"

"I mean, we had a chance in high school. But I feel like now, he doesn't really understand much about what's important to me. He basically told me not to finish my doctorate! And for all his talk about how important the museum is, he hasn't actually wanted to donate."

Emi was silent for a minute. "Did he actually tell you not to finish your degree? And what was the rationale?"

Aya thought back to it. The conversation had been overshadowed by the events in the reading room but not quite obliterated. "I don't know. There were lots of reasons. But I think it says something that you came out here specifically to tell me to finish my degree, and he tried to convince me not to listen to you."

Emi smiled. "So you saw through my excuses, huh?"

Aya rolled her eyes. "You came back home for a visit when your parents weren't even here? Um, yes, Dr. Obvious. Safe to say I saw through that one."

Emi pulled herself up, wiggled down from the bed, and hugged her. "So that's it? You're just going to give him up?"

Aya frowned, straightening the pearl necklace she had borrowed from her mom. "Of course not. I'm going to try to make it work."

"Because..."

"Because I've never felt this way about anyone else," Aya answered. "And that has to mean something."

"Okay," said Emi cautiously. "If you've never felt this way before, do you think Noah knows that?"

Aya scoffed. "Probably. I mean, my love life this past decade has been pretty pathetic. You've seen it."

"But he hasn't. He might imagine you don't really feel that much for him these days."

Aya laughed. "Oh, okay. He's a celebrity, Emi. He thinks everyone is madly in love with him."

"Does he, though?"

Aya rolled her eyes. "The annoying thing is that he's right."

47

————

Noah

Noah stood in front of a line full of temporary workers.

Grace was good at rallying the troops, efficient but ruthlessly so. People always respected her without quite knowing why. And Amanda, the temporary site manager, had an ease of manner that made you know instantly she was a pro. Her hair might have been dyed a strange shade of pink, but if anything, that just enhanced her credibility. She didn't even have to raise her voice to give instructions.

The stages were all set up, even the one that the crew had struggled with the day before. Lots of barriers had been set up along the outside, and the main entrance and exit had huge signs in place. The first aid tent was ready, trailers were waiting for temperamental musicians, and they had scanners for the tickets and backup scanners in case those failed. And since Noah was there, in front of the main stage, his very presence caused excitement and whispers in the ranks.

But there was a piece missing.

"So," Grace said. "What's happening with the food trucks? The maps you gave me didn't show them."

Noah looked around. The temporary site didn't have a good place for them. If they had been able to use the fairgrounds as originally planned, there would have been lots of space for the picnic tables and the food. But in the current location, they were either going to have to cancel that part of the event or think of a creative solution.

Though there was a bit of a breeze, the weather was warm, sunny but without humidity, so it wasn't going to be incredibly hot. In two and a half days, the festival would be in full swing, and everyone who was shuffling in the crowd before him would be run off their feet, making things happen. It should have been a proud moment for Noah. After all, though he'd released an insane number of albums and worked a ton of hours in many jobs, he'd never brought people together like that. He remembered how Nami had given him the idea a year and a half ago, just when he needed something new to boost his confidence. His sister had some great ideas.

"Noah," said Grace. "What's it going to be? People need to eat."

"I know. One s-second."

Of course, it was technically possible to get to the town of Love Hollow from where they were. But they were all counting on the festivalgoers being a captive audience. You wouldn't expect a baseball fan to leave the stadium, miss the game, and go get a better deal on fries in some fast food joint a mile away. Music fans were similar. They might not mind tapping their feet and humming as they waited in a line, but they wouldn't want to go off-site for food, especially since the parking situation was going to be tricky at best.

He stood frozen, listening to the workers speaking, and

wondered if he would have to address them. Grace and Amanda were supposed to be helping him avoid stuttering in front of a crowd.

Grace handed him a document, which fluttered in the wind. He knew what it said even before he saw it.

"I thought you wanted me to handle things," he said.

"This is one way of handling it," she murmured. "Otherwise, with no food? That's it for us, financially speaking."

Noah sighed. In many ways, the festival was no different from the events he used to be forced to volunteer for, back when he was an A-Wing kid in high school. Sure, it was all well and good that neighboring cities brought their marching bands to the "Bonanza of the Bands"—someone had complained that "Battle of the Bands" was unwelcoming. But it wasn't really about all the bands playing their bizarre versions of pop hits. It was about the nachos that the visiting band members, their parents, and their bedraggled younger siblings purchased. Those nachos funded the Love Hollow High band budget for the coming year. Without the food, the event was worthless.

That was going to be the case for the festival too. They simply couldn't afford to skimp on the food trucks. Still, he hesitated.

"Is this going to cause problems for you?" asked Grace. "Do you want us to wait for a minute while you call Aya?"

He looked down at his phone. She could have texted him back. Instead, she hadn't even responded to confirm whether she needed a ride to Nobu's engagement party.

"No," he said. "This is going to work. It has to."

48

T he Katos' home was overflowing with people. Half of them, Aya didn't even know. The glamour they exuded indicated they were probably friends of Nobu and Justin, yuppies who had flown in from Denver for the event and would be nursing their hangovers the next day with iced coffee as they went antique shopping and gushed over Love Hollow's "quaint" series of shops in its historic downtown. Most of them were in outfits that were both more expensive and less fancy than hers. Cocktail attire encompassed a wider range of clothing than she'd thought.

Then there were the people Aya did know. She caught sight of Carson Cobb. Apparently, black was an appropriate color, and it looked really good on Carson. It accentuated the blond in her hair. Carson's dress had one of those necklines that would never work on Aya. She could never even remember the name. It went all the way down past Carson's pierced belly button. Aya had heard dresses like that had to be held on with some kind of tape, which had always seemed painful to her. But seeing Carson, she could see why people went for it.

Noah was going for it, apparently. He was standing in a corner, clinking glasses with Carson and taking big swigs of champagne. Her laughter was audible even over the noise of the crowd. Aya didn't know what to say to either of them, so she attempted to escape to the kitchen, where Nami was wearing an emerald-green dress underneath a sweatshirt.

"Hi," said Aya.

Nami raised her eyebrows. "Hey. "I thought you'd be too busy to come."

"No. I mean, things are busy, but I didn't want to miss this."

Nami's smile was strained as she whisked an impossibly small spoon through a little glass container of soup and rice. Hana, in her high chair, was adorable. Aya was glad to see that she could look at the baby and not think too much about Byron. Hana had probably gotten some features from both parents, but with her round face and lopsided grin, she really just looked like herself.

"You and Noah are funny," Nami said. "Miss all the baby stuff but go to the engagement party, huh?"

When Aya didn't respond, Nami shook her head.

"It's okay. I mean, not for him but for you. Twyla says you're basically a hermit these days, so I shouldn't take it personally."

Aya frowned, hoping Nami wasn't referring to the gender reveal and shower that had preceded Hana's birth. She had felt a little guilty about skipping them and only rationalized it by deciding that it would be rude to show up without a gift. And she couldn't afford a gift, so problem solved.

"I go out of town at least every other week, so I don't think I am," said Aya.

"Yeah, but for work stuff, right? Everyone in my family is like that too. Don't know how I ended up the only one not married to the job."

They could hear Nobu's loud voice over the crowd and the pop of champagne.

"Is Nobu really married to the job?" Aya asked.

Nami gave her daughter another spoonful. "Yes. You'd be surprised. He's just good at taking advantage of his weeks and hours away. He's a lot like Dad in that regard."

"Not your mom, though?"

Nami scoffed. "Mom almost brought a pile of grading to my wedding."

Their mother swept into the kitchen. "I spent so much time helping you with the details of those hideous flower arrangements that I had to do at least a little grading. Since you insisted on having your wedding during the school year."

Aya shifted in her chair, not sure how much she was supposed to say about Nami's wedding. *Wouldn't talking about that bring back all sorts of memories of Byron?* But neither of the Kato women seemed discomfited. Mrs. Kato was at the sink, adding water to a large pitcher full of ice and cucumbers, Nami was grinning at the baby, and little Hana was slapping her hands down on the tray of the high chair.

"I'm sorry I missed it," Aya mumbled. She couldn't remember what excuse she had given at the time, but she had felt a little bit guilty. Now that the Kato family was older, her dogged avoidance of events where Noah might be present had made things ever more awkward.

Of course, going to an event where Noah was present wasn't any guarantee against awkwardness. Mrs. Kato had left the door to the dining room open, and Noah was sitting in a circle full of women she didn't recognize. He was drinking the cocktail Nobu had insisted on mixing himself, some sort of hit with his friends in Denver. He called it a "D-Minus in a Glass," and from the shade of Noah's cheeks, it looked rather strong.

"Aya," said Nami. "It's seriously great that you missed it. Big white wedding? Done. Check."

"Yeah. Okay. But I am sorry to have missed the baby stuff."

Nami shook her head again. "Twy and Marty were there for me. And your mom. I'd say your family was working triple time."*

That only made Aya feel worse. She remembered how much her mother had encouraged her to just do one thing for Nami, to try to cheer her up, to go hold the baby for twenty minutes, but she had refused. She hadn't wanted to deal with Noah's family, and she was also afraid of the messiness of the situation. She usually avoided people who were not feeling happy, afraid of exposing her own mental weaknesses. Even with Emi, she had hesitated before booking a flight. She had gone eventually, though. Her poor friend, who had never known heartbreak, had really been sucked into a vortex of despair. Back before Charles, Emi had gotten her heart so badly broken on her backpacking trip to China that Aya had known it was her duty to be there. Yet she had tried to get out of it.

"I'm sorry," Aya said suddenly.

Nami put the spoon down and looked directly at her. "It's okay. But don't keep repeating your mistake."

"What?"

"Get out there. Enjoy the party."

Aya tried to follow Nami's advice. She got a little bit

closer to Noah, but that only forced her into the crowd of admirers who had gathered around him. She was in the outer ring with a couple of the best-looking women she had ever seen. Their names were Diana and Mimi, and they wore matching gold jumpsuits that looked like they must be seventies vintage but were in such great condition that Aya suspected they had been tailor-made for them.

Her phone buzzed with a picture. She had tried to tell herself she wouldn't do work things all evening, but she was relieved to see it, even when she saw that the sender was Mrs. Irving. *When did Mrs. Irving learn to send text messages?* It was going to be even more difficult to dodge her.

Of course, the message wasn't exactly clear. Mrs. Irving's thumb covered half the picture, and what remained wasn't in perfect focus. But Aya had seen enough. She put her drink down and wiped her palms on a napkin.

"I'm so excited for the festival," Diana said before Aya could escape. "I've been wanting to go talk to Noah all evening, but I can't bring myself to do it! It's crazy. Nobu is so nice, but I just never thought I'd be near a celebrity like this."

Mimi, who was Diana's wife, rolled her eyes. "Yes, well, Nobu would remind you that his brother is the less handsome version of himself. Et cetera, et cetera."

Diana took another swig of champagne. "Oh, Noah is so dreamy, though! He looks like a taller, handsomer Nobu. Don't tell him I said that!"

Aya shifted in her chair.

Mimi shrugged. "Ah, the celebrity crushes. It could be worse. All of mine are athletes. So put me in a room full of killer basketball players and women's soccer stars, and I'll look like just as much of an idiot."

"I am *not* an idiot," Diana insisted, giving her wife a playful swat.

Aya gave a wan smile. She hated being the third wheel with couples who were bickering, but when they flirted in front of her, it was even more annoying.

She excused herself then sidled up to Noah. "I need your help. Can I talk to you outside for a minute?"

Aya spoke in Japanese, as that was the only way they were going to get any semblance of privacy. Their Japanese lessons with their grandparents had been fairly ad hoc, though Aya had taken a couple of semesters in college. Plus, she had years of experience speaking with Emi's parents. Noah clearly did not understand much anymore, especially not when he was drunk.

"Nani?" he asked, grinning at her.

"Outside," Aya said through gritted teeth.

49

———

N oah
"Noah, the festival is about to start. Grace told me to talk to you. The museum grounds are crawling with food trucks."

His stomach fell. "It's a temporary lease. We cleared it with one of your board members this morning."

"Did you think to call me?" Aya demanded.

"I did. But I didn't want you to say no."

Aya's voice was stony. "Let me guess. Mrs. Irving thought it would be a great idea for our entire event to smell like cheap tacos."

"She's a r-reasonable person, Aya! If you talk to her. She had been calling me nonstop."

"Okay." Aya's voice had dropped in volume and was steady—scarily steady. "So, I take it you were going to tell me sometime? Because this is a pretty big lie of omission."

He felt compelled to defend himself. "I tried to say something earlier," he hissed. "Then I forgot, and I had to rush out. What was I supposed to do?"

"I mean, you could have knocked on my door! You never said you had work stuff you wanted to talk about!"

"Oh, okay," he said, thinking furiously. "So I can talk to you whenever as long as it's about work stuff? Because when I text about anything else, you don't get back to me."

"I thought I was your plus-one for this event!" she cried. "And you've been ignoring me all night!"

"People asked me to play guitar," he said, shocked that she would have a problem with it. "It's the only thing I can do for Nobu and Justin that's special, okay? They both prefer Nami to me, and Mom and Dad are already annoyed because I've missed so many family things. Just for once, I wanted to have this experience. With my family."

"Then why did you even ask me? I didn't need to be here."

"Justin told me to," he said. It wasn't exactly a lie, although it certainly wasn't the whole truth. He had asked her because he wanted to spend time with her. And because, secretly, he did consider her a part of his family.

But he wasn't about to say that.

"Ooh, Justin," Aya said. "So he's important enough to get me invited, but I don't qualify on my own merits?"

The academic language threw him. "I'm sorry. What?"

"No. Noah, I should have known. The tabloids were right all along."

"They're never right." he said.

"They got the story right," she said quietly. "Your story. Sure, some of those women, that was just for show. I get that now. But the gist of what they were saying, that you just use women, that you're too passionate about your musical reputation to commit to anything? That part was true."

"You have no idea how lonely it is," he shot back.

She shook her head, and her voice quavered when she answered. "Ordinary people are lonely too, Noah. And sad and frustrated and suffering. You don't get a monopoly on that just by living in a shallow, dysfunctional fishbowl."

They were interrupted by Nobu. He came out with two large glasses of wine, and it finally hit Noah that they could probably be heard from the kitchen.

"Hi, lovebirds," he said. "I may not be a married man quite yet, but I can tell you a good toast fixes a lot. Noah, maybe take whatever you were going to use for the wedding and get it all out now, huh?"

Aya glared. "You shouldn't be defending him. Your family needed him, and he's never around."

Nobu shrugged. "We're getting by, Aya. We always thought Noah would end up back here eventually, and here he is, eh?"

Aya took the glass from Nobu, but she didn't drink.

Noah refused to take a glass. "Dude, in case you haven't noticed, you don't live here either."

"Yes, but he's been here," Aya shot back. "Do you have any idea how hard things have been for Nami? Everyone in your family was rallying around her. Hell, my own mom took food over every week."

Noah didn't say anything. Hana had a funny little book collection full of babyish biographies of famous feminists and board books about impressionist paintings. His mother had said they came "from the *Hanson* home," which seemed to mean they were gifts from Aya. She hadn't taken credit for it, though. *Did she pick out all those beautiful books because Nami was suffering?*

"She has a lot of help," said Noah weakly.

Aya sucked in a breath.

"So postpartum depression is fine as long as you have *help*. That's good to know."

Nobu shook his head, taking a large swig from the wineglass. "Fuck, this is good. Aya, don't listen to him. He's not in the loop. Mom and Dad thought we had to shield him from the worst of it, as things have been so rough with his record company this past year."

"Things have... Where are you getting that from?" Noah asked.

Nobu gave him a tight-lipped smile. "Oh, my dear boy. I read the papers, too, you know."

Aya stood like a statue in her peach dress. She looked beautiful with the wineglass in her hand, the gentle light of the late-day sun splashing across her features. But she looked miserable too.

"I'm sorry, Noah," she said. "I can't give up everything in my life just to be your temporary side piece."

"That's n-not what I'm asking," Noah said.

"What are you asking again?" asked Nobu, seeming confused.

"Nothing! I'm not asking for anything, dammit."

Aya nodded. She took a sip of her wine before handing it back to Nobu. "It's good, but I have to drive myself back home."

A long silence followed as she walked down to her car. As she drove away, Nobu looked over at Noah.

"You want to walk to the creek or something? I don't have the shoes for it, but I'll indulge you if you shine these for me afterward."

Noah gave a tremulous laugh. "Don't you need to get back in there?"

Nobu shrugged. "I got out the better shiraz. Have you

tried it? It's really very good. I'd say I've done my part for the moment."

Shoving a glass at his brother, he started up the path. And Noah decided to follow.

50

———

"Do you remember Joseph Park?" asked Nobu.

He was ambling along, and Noah struggled not to run. He was so angry that he felt like he should go for a jog to get all the emotions out of his system.

"Sure. The only other Asian kid in your grade. Unlike me, you and Aya always had people to hang out with."

Nobu laughed a little without really smiling. "You, too, Noah? I didn't hang out with Joseph because he was the only other Asian kid. I hung around him because I thought he was hot."

Noah wrinkled his nose. "Joseph *Park*?"

At that, Nobu gave a genuine laugh. "Listen to you! You looked pretty awkward in high school yourself."

"Okay. Justin is way hotter, though."

Nobu raised his eyebrows. "I agree. Anyway, senior year, I finally told Joseph how I felt."

"Okay." Noah tried to remember whether he had noticed anything going on with Nobu during that time, but he'd been so fixated on his own unimpressive grades that his siblings' emotional lives were a blank.

Nobu sighed. "Supposedly, he felt the same. And we were going to the same college, so I thought we were set."

Noah squinted, trying to see Nobu's expression in the fading light. "So what the hell happened? Broke up in college?"

"He got a girlfriend once we got there," said Nobu shortly. "It was like the whole thing had never happened."

Noah took a sip of his wine. "This feels like some sort of parable, dude. You're going to have to spell it out for me."

"I thought Aya shouldn't get too attached to you and that you shouldn't expect anything from Aya," he said.

Noah snorted. "Yeah, and you were right."

"No," he said firmly. "I was wrong. And I take responsibility for that, even though you two were idiots for listening to me."

Noah thought back. He might have been completely oblivious to how Nobu was feeling during those years, but he remembered his own painful insecurity. Nobu had warned him that Aya wouldn't want anything serious, and he'd believed that without question.

"You're not responsible for how things are now," said Noah finally. "I could have reached out to her. I also could have come home more often, and I just didn't."

Nobu was silent.

"Do you think Nami will forgive me?" Noah asked. He didn't dare ask about Aya. Her forgiveness seemed impossible.

Nobu grinned. "You might be the most famous, but Nami will always be the most impressive of all of us."

Noah nodded. "Yeah, I know. So what does that mean?"

"It means you should at least give it a shot."

51

———

Aya

Aya swam a lot when she was staying with Emi and Charles. Emi was like a sister to Aya, but Charles was virtually a stranger. The weather in Santa Cruz was so mild that it shocked her. Emi's street of suburban mansions was the very definition of quiet. At first, it was as if Aya had been transported to an alien landscape, as if Love Hollow had never existed.

When Aya was swimming, she didn't have to think about how she had abandoned her beloved museum. Mrs. Irving, who was uncharacteristically sympathetic, had insisted she would work everything out. Aya didn't have faith that things would go well, but when forced to choose between the museum and her PhD, she had firmly checked "none of the above." The option she had chosen was to cry in a darkened room, hand over the Pilgrimage responsibilities to her mother and sister, and think about how her flirtation with Noah had cost her the best job of her life.

Eventually, Emi carted Aya off to California. It was better, Emi explained, to have a change of scene. And indeed, Aya stopped crying once she was in California. She ate and swam and slept. It was as if she had paused her life and crawled into an uncommonly pretty screensaver. Pool. Lounge chairs. Sunshine.

The only way she knew that time was passing was the size and shape of Emi's belly. By early August, it looked notably puffy, though Emi still insisted that it would look normal under a loose white coat. She needed to feel that it would, anyway, because her job was starting in September and she didn't want to tell anyone there just yet. Emi might be working at a nonprofit clinic, but the general societal attitudes about pregnant women would still be in play.

"What did you really think back in high school?" Aya asked one night. They were drinking coconut water and relaxing on pool noodles, and the beauty of the sunset made Aya feel drunk. Which made a change—for weeks, she had hardly felt anything.

"Seriously?" asked Emi. "You're sure you want to know?"

"Yes."

"I thought you and Noah would be together forever," Emi said thoughtfully. "Grandkids, shared room in the nursing home. All of it."

Aya pushed her noodle down and tried to stand on it. The awkwardness of her efforts to balance meant she didn't have to look at Emi. "You never said that, though."

Out of the corner of her eye, she could see that Emi was giving her a wry smile.

"Well, I was going to wait until you started officially dating. Then when that didn't happen, I kept quiet."

Aya gave a sad smile. "I didn't want to risk all that, you know? At least, not until prom night. But really, not even then."

"With what happened in your parents' marriage, I don't blame you."

Aya pushed the noodles aside. "I don't think anyone has a perfect marriage. But Mom and Daddy?"

"No," said Emi. "That's not what I'm saying. Your lives were ripped apart when he died. I can imagine how hard it would be to…"

Aya frowned. "What? To have a good life?"

Emi took a sip of her coconut water. "That's not what I said."

Several more moments went by. Anger bubbled up within Aya then fizzled out almost as quickly. It was something Emi had told her about—noticing emotions, naming them, then letting them go. Apparently, according to Emi, there were randomized controlled trials. Doctors dispensed advice like that to their patients, though fortunately, Aya had never been forced to endure a lecture on mindfulness by some guru in a white coat. Throughout her life, Aya had been suspicious of the American advice to express emotions. In her household, she had her mother and her younger sisters around. If she didn't hold it together, who knew what would happen to them.

But she had started to practice, very occasionally, at Emi's urging. After all, she had to do something in exchange for the fancy guest room, the pool, and the excellent food that she picked at.

"So you think I didn't want to fall in love because I was scared that Noah would leave me? Because I felt like, by dying, my dad had abandoned us?" Aya's throat closed as she said it. "That sounds like some crazy psychobabble to me," she managed.

"Look," said Emi. "I don't want to blame you. Or Noah. But if you're already mad at me, I did have one question."

Aya looked her in the eye. "What's that?"

"What are you going to do with the rest of your life?"

52

Aya took a pile of papers home for Christmas. She'd been warned by her colleagues. "Always have due dates after the holidays," they'd said. "That way, you can enjoy the time off without having stacks of papers to grade." According to them, it was one of the perks of the quarter system, which meant their grades weren't due until the second week of January.

But Aya hadn't listened. Freshmen—or first-year students, as she was supposed to call them—were such novices in terms of both their writing and their critical analysis. And they seemed to think Aya wouldn't be able to pick out the essays that had been written by machines. She'd taken to having the students write an essay each day during class time. The last twenty minutes of class were set aside for the students to make the revisions she suggested in the margins of the essays they had written the class before. It meant that there was very little time for lecturing, but Aya found that she didn't mind. The students were more engaged for the fifteen minutes she spent speaking, as they knew they had to write about the topic right after. And her methods, though unorthodox, seemed to be working. Her students were getting more interested in primary sources, and their arguments finally had some specificity. It had been weeks since any of them tried to start an essay by quoting the dictionary definition of a historical term.

But it did mean that Aya had so many essays to get through on her flights that she couldn't even think about Christmas in Love Hollow until Martha picked her up at the airport.

"Don't drive on the left," Aya said as she hugged her sister. Martha had gone to Japan to teach English after college and never left.

"*Daijoubu, yo*," teased Martha. "I'll do half and half. I'll start by driving on the left but only for a few miles."

"How are you even driving me anyway?" grumbled Aya. "Aren't you too jet-lagged?"

Martha scoffed. Normally, her voice was a little more high-pitched than Twyla's, a strange difference that had only been accentuated by Martha's time in Japan. But when she was sarcastic, she sounded just like her twin. "I've been home for ten days, and I was in recital mode half the time."

Aya squirmed. She could have come home well before Christmas Eve if she hadn't had so much work to do on her dissertation.

"Sorry I missed it."

Martha grinned. "Twy and I had it covered. And our duet *killed*. That's why I got this haircut."

She pushed at her cute little bob. In Love Hollow, Martha and Twyla could have passed for about fourteen with that hair. In Japan, Aya guessed that people were probably much better at guessing her sister's real age.

"You really need to stop trying to trick those poor kids, Marty."

"But it's *so* fun. What's the point of having an identical twin if you never use it to prank anyone?"

The landscape was beautiful, fresh snow under a blue sky. Aya drank it in through the car windows. "Big-sky country," she murmured.

Martha laughed. "Yeah, it's big. I think Montana got the slogan, though, not Idaho."

"Don't you miss it?"

"Not really. But it looks nice today."

53

Aya

Aya and Martha arrived home to an empty house. Twyla was working, and their mother was still organizing the costumes she had used for the annual Christmas spectacular. The recital was a great deal of work, which was why Aya didn't usually miss it.

"I have some work to do," announced Martha, bringing out a sleek little laptop. "You're making dinner, right?"

Aya nodded. "I can, but it's still afternoon."

Martha began humming. "We're low on ingredients," she said. "You should go to the Radner's now if you want to get anything. Otherwise, there will be basically nothing to put in the ramen."

Christmas ramen was a Hanson tradition. Though it had begun in the early years, when three children under the age of four made it difficult for Aya's parents to get anything on the table, it became a dish they loved fiercely. It involved instant noodles, broth made from scratch, and lots of red and green add-ins that weren't terribly traditional—sautéed red, green, and yellow peppers, kimchi whenever they had it, and boiled eggs dyed red and green.

Aya passed the museum on the way to the store. She knew it was still open somehow, but she didn't have any of the details. Talking about it with her mother and sisters was taboo, and she was glad they hadn't shared anything. But a few cars were in the parking lot, and she was intrigued. Usually, they closed for the whole holiday season, shutting down days before Christmas and not opening up until well into the new year. Certainly, they were never open on Christmas Eve. But it looked like several people were there.

Aya tried not to think about it. Her guilt over abandoning the museum, while it had lessened over time, would probably never really go away. She turned carefully into the Radner's parking lot, making sure to stay close to the exit so it would be easy for her to get out.

By the time she finished her shopping, which she did hastily to avoid any Kato family members who might be present, it had started to snow again. And there were many more cars in the parking lot of the museum. She found herself turning in, drawn to the front doors by the attractive decorations. The night was absolutely freezing, so the groceries would be fine for a bit in her trunk.

Ella Chang, Noah's musician friend, was dressed in a formfitting red dress with white trim and greeted her with a hug.

"Oh hi," said Aya. "Are you here for the holidays?"

Ella looked mystified. "Um, I live here?"

"Okay. I didn't know that."

Ella frowned. "Anyway, I'm not going to ask you for a ticket. You can go through to the theater."

"Theater," muttered Aya, making her way through the

people standing around with wineglasses and canapés. "That's an interesting choice of words."

The main exhibition room really didn't have great acoustics, and it seemed a bit of a stretch to call the place a theater. They only used it for events because there was no other choice.

But at the end of the room, there were two doors. They didn't use to be there, but as people were filtering through them, Aya realized there was a new room there—an actual theater.

As she walked through, some snatches of conversation came back to her. Generally, Aya didn't interact much with scholars who studied the exact same thing she did. She worked with a lot of people who studied American history, but it was rare for her to speak to someone else directly researching the same internment camps. But one such scholar had passed through her campus only a few weeks ago, as they were going to a conference nearby, and they made some mystifying remarks about big donations to museums that were working to preserve the internment sites.

Aya had hardly paid attention at the time. In fact, she'd been annoyed, as she remembered how much she'd had to beg for money as a museum director. But judging by the size of this recently completed building addition, she realized some sort of sizable donation must have been made.

"Good evening," said a beautiful woman to the assembled crowd. "How's everyone doing this evening?"

Aya had to blink several times before she realized the beautiful entertainer was, in fact, Nami. Ella quickly joined her on stage, but it would have been hard to say who looked more glamorous. Nami was wearing a long green cocktail dress, and her hair was in a wavy bob reminiscent of a 1920s starlet.

Aya couldn't help but smile. Twyla had gotten a bob, then Martha had followed. If Nami had been next, there must be a clear trend happening in Love Hollow.

"As you know," Nami said, "we have done some very impressive fundraising to create this beautiful space."

The crowd cheered.

"I'm sure you all know that some of our largest donations ended up being well into seven figures!"

More cheering followed, and Nami grinned, but her face then became serious. "But those are the kind of things we can't rely on," she said. "And none of it is as important as the work we are still doing in this town."

The crowd was quiet, and Nami continued. "Our shared history is here, and our future is here too," she said. "When Love Hollow students stopped coming, when we were slandered in the newspapers, it exposed work that we had neglected for years. That's why all the proceeds from tonight are going to the Field Trip Fund."

More cheers erupted, but Nami waved them down. "If there are any of you who don't know, that means that once we have everything we need for this fund, we will never have to charge for field trips again. In fact, we will be able to help pay for transportation for kids who want to come here, starting with Love Hollow kids but eventually including children from all over the country."

The applause went on so long that Nami had to gesture to the crowd to keep it down.

"But that's only part of the reason you're here tonight," she said. "We sold lots of tickets because of my brother's willingness to perform. Here he is, the one and only Noah Kato!"

54

———

Noah

    Noah was surprised by the crowd. He'd thought he had retreated fairly well, hanging back after the release of his first independent album, but apparently, his reputation as a recluse had made him more popular than ever—which was ironic. Because Noah, for the first time, had been learning to accept stuttering. After decades of trying to avoid it, it didn't come naturally. But he'd hired a crazy speech therapist who emphasized speech, not the endless quest to be stutter-free, and it was helping.

For the first time ever, Noah Kato hadn't rehearsed his banter. He didn't try to avoid certain words or speak in a weirdly singsong way. He just spoke.

"I thought a lot about w-what to play tonight," he said. For what happened next, he told himself he was "blocking" —that weird thing that happened when he stuttered and couldn't get a word out. He would try to speak but couldn't.

But that wasn't what actually happened. He saw Aya sitting in the aisle, near the back. Usually, it was impossible to make out faces beyond the first few rows, but he knew she was there.

And in that instant, he changed the song.

"Black is the Color of My True Love's Hair" was the only possible choice. He meant it even more than he had back in high school, and he found himself wishing she would come to the front and join him—Aya, with her melodious voice that soothed his nerves and made him believe in his own musicality.

Of course, she didn't join him. But that didn't mean he was going to let her go.

He sensed her leaving as he finished his set, which included rushing through a bare-bones cover of "Always" by Irving Berlin and the one original he'd chosen, "Remember (Please)." The last song, which had been a hit on his solo album, was written about her. And he was fairly sure she knew that.

There was plenty of applause, but some of that was for Ella. She was a star in her own right, and her move back to Love Hollow had garnered a lot of attention.

Plus, her electric guitar was really lighting up the crowd.

Noah caught up with Aya when she was almost at the door. She'd already put on her coat.

"Wait," he said.

She turned back but only to give a small smile.

The catering staff was milling around, setting up for the reception. There was a lot of food. With the amount they were charging for tickets, there had to be.

"Can I talk to you?" asked Noah.

"Shall we talk in the office?" She was blinking back tears.

He looked at the door to Nami's office, which had once been Aya's. He could tell she was also thinking of the last time they had been there—together.

"Sure," said Noah. He was more nervous than he had been in years, yet he wasn't stuttering at all. That was the thing about his stutter—it just came and went.

But that didn't mean he was going to have an easy time finding the words.

"I'm sorry," he said as soon as they were in the office. They'd closed the door but both stood near it. In fact, Aya's hand was still on the handle, as if she were ready to escape.

Since Aya didn't answer, Noah went on. "I should have made you a priority. I wanted the festival to go well, but I cared so much more about you. I never admitted it, though."

Aya hesitated. "You didn't really act like either."

"No. I didn't. And honestly, I wasn't sure how you felt."

Aya looked around the office, taking in the new furniture and updated computers. "Did you donate all this?"

He scratched his head. "I know a lot of people in LA. And I was so depressed after you left that I wrote a pretty decent album."

She gave a tiny smile. "Decent? I heard it grossed millions."

"Yeah," said Noah. "So I tried to do all the fundraising I could, then I came here to set up a studio."

Aya frowned. "Twyla told me something about a studio, but I thought it was only Ella's," she said. "Making Love Hollow the next Muscle Shoals or something like that?"

"Something like that."

A pause followed.

"The festival was stupid, really," said Noah. "I just wanted to do something that would help my family. But a one-week event is nothing. If you're committed, you stay."

Aya took a deep breath. When she spoke, she was the one stuttering. "I w-wanted to be with you," she said. "But I still didn't believe you wanted me in the same way."

Noah took a step backward, shocked. "You didn't believe that?"

She shook her head. "I mean, as a side piece, sure. But I felt like, here I am, fat, broke, never having finished anything."

Noah gasped. "Aya, you're the most beautiful woman I've ever met! And you're a genius!"

That made her laugh, and she stepped away from the door, swatting Noah on the arm. "Oh, come on."

Frowning, he said, "I'm serious. I've always been serious about you."

He could see that Aya was trying to think of a response, but she didn't say anything.

Instead, she kissed him.

All of Noah's doubts fell away. In that kiss, he felt her love and the urgency of coming together after such a long separation. Her hands were buried in his hair, and he found himself longing to pick her up, to carry her away from the drab office that no longer seemed able to contain them.

When they broke apart, Aya asked him a question.

"Would you like to come over tomorrow for a Hanson Christmas feast?"

Her eyes were twinkling. She wasn't crying anymore.

But Noah wasn't ready to joke. "Yes," he said. "Also, would you marry me?"

55

EPILOGUE

Nami's room reeked of hairspray. Aya, wearing a red silk dress, sat in front of the mirror as her mother put the finishing touches on her hair.

Red wasn't a conventional choice for a bride, but she loved the dress.

"I would've helped you get some shoes that actually matched," her mother muttered. "But there wasn't an opportunity!"

Aya grinned. "We were only engaged for a week, Mom. That didn't exactly give you a lot of time."

"I suppose a lot of those wedding preparations are a waste of time anyway." Her voice was still muffled by the bobby pins in her mouth.

"You wouldn't have wanted me to diet?"

It slipped out. Aya never talked to her mother about weight.

She cocked her head. "Why would I ever ask you to diet, Aya?"

The truth hung between them. In the past week, through many conversations with both Noah and her friends, Aya had started to unpack how she felt about her body. But she had never told her mom.

"It felt weird that you didn't let me do the pageants," said Aya. "Like I wasn't skinny or pretty enough, but Twyla and Martha did all of them."

"I never wanted any of you to do them!" said her mother, incredulous. "And you were the firstborn, so I stuck to my guns."

Aya frowned. "I always figured you let the twins do them because they were skinny."

"They wore me down," her mother said, shaking her head. "Begging me for months, whining constantly. You know how they are when they decide to be a team. And I still regret it! Do you know what one of the other parents said to Twyla before Miss Love Hollow?"

Aya shook her head.

"This is the age when a lot of girls start getting big thighs," said Aya's mother, breathless with rage. "Can you imagine?"

Aya *could* imagine it. She had hated her own thighs for ages, refusing to wear shorts or anything but the longest skirts, never feeling at ease even when her legs were toned and strong.

"I've always been protective of you girls. And I didn't want to tell you how pretty you were all the time. Because then I thought you would think about looks too much! I wanted you to have the joy of ballet without all that insecurity."

She was crying, and Aya passed her a tissue. Fortunately, there were plenty on hand.

"I feel beautiful today," said Aya, and it was the truth.

A knock sounded on the door.

"Come in!" said her mother.

Nami entered. "I'm about to walk Hana down," she said, kissing her baby's hair. "Time for you both to get out there."

Aya stood, taking her mother's arm.

They walked out of Nami's room and down the hallway. It was only about ten feet, but everyone stood, even Ella, who had her guitar.

The Katos' living room was packed with people. Martha and Twyla were standing at the front with Nobu, Nami, Hana, and Justin, who was officiating. And Noah's smile was so radiant that Aya could hardly look at him.

The Katos, soon to be Aya's parents-in-law, were off to the side. The Chang family stood with them. Chen and Sheena had come all the way from California, and they had a phone pulled up with Emi on it.

"Dearly beloved," intoned Justin as Aya took Noah's hand.

They couldn't stop grinning at each other. Finally, they'd gotten it right.

Author's Note

Be sure and check out the Bonus Epilogue at https://dl. bookfunnel.com/6o4tafxro5. It's only available here!

Love Hollow, that charming little town, does not actually exist. There is no interment camp there, and it is not based on any real or fictional place.

Japanese-American interment, however, is all too real.

I'm part of the same generation as Aya and Noah. One of my grandparents was in an internment camp with other Japanese-American young people, and it's hard to overstate the impact that has on a person's life. It has an influence on future generations, too, though that is more subtle.

If you've ever visited Washington, DC, you may have seen the memorial to people who were in these internment camps. Most likely, though, you missed it. It's off the beaten path, not quite on the National Mall, not overly close to the main sights. After all, not everyone wants to be reminded of this shameful chapter in America's history, and it might be awkward if it were *too* near the memorial to the FDR. After all, he was responsible.

One day, I went to great lengths to see this memorial. My kids were with me, both young enough to sleep in a stroller, and I started thinking about all of the people who were in different camps. When I passed the name of the camp where my relatives were, I started to cry. I was overcome with emotion, thinking about both the tragedy of the circumstances and the resilience of the people who endured them.

And then I noticed that one of the camps was called Heart Mountain.

Now, is it just me, or is that the PERFECT name for a romance novel? Alas, I have never actually visited Heart Mountain, and I didn't want to slander the people who lived there. Plus, the museum seemed to be doing pretty well. So my husband came up with the name "Love Hollow" and this project was born.

Thank you for reading, and please stay tuned for the next installments in this series! Don't worry, Emi will eventually get the attention she deserves.

Until next time,

Eve MT